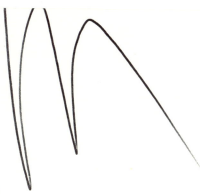

THE BIG EASY

THE
BIG
EASY

THE NOVEL

JAMES CONAWAY

SECOND EDITION
originally published by Houghton Mifflin

Copyright © 2014 by James Conaway

CONAWAY BOOKS

in association with Fearless Assisted Publishing
www.fearlessbooks.com/Conaway.htm

———————————————

This book is a work of fiction. Names, characters, places, and
incidents either are products of the author's imagination or are
used fictitiously. Any resemblance to actual events or locales
or persons, living or dead, is entirely coincidental.

———————————————

ISBN: 978-0-9897255-0-7

LIBRARY OF CONGRESS CONTROL NO.:
2013923814

DESIGN, TYPOGRAPHY, AND PRODUCTION:

D. Patrick Miller, Fearless Literary Services
www.fearlessbooks.com/Literary.html

AUTHOR PHOTO BY
Peter Menzel

TABLE OF CONTENTS

For PENNY

Do I really *want* to be integrated into a burning house?

— James Baldwin, *The Fire Next Time*

PART 1:

Oh, the Smell of Her

RIDING ACROSS TOWN to the cemetery, Comiski fell asleep. It was total abandonment, inevitable and noisy, undisturbed by the cab's maneuvers through early morning traffic: the sleep of a man deprived of rest and, curiously, of pride — he was too vulnerable. The web of his dreams was fragile and inconclusive, censored by his arrival; he woke up drained, faced with a sagging iron gate and a moraine of low mausoleums.

The grounds were strewn with Dixie beer cans, scraps of newspaper, discarded contraceptives — the residue of what might have been his own forgotten revels. He wandered myopically among the decaying tributes to the dead, touching the impressions left by brass plaques long since pried away, the broken wings of stone angels; tried to remember why he had come. Spreading water oaks cut him off from the sun, their roots splitting a wall of honeycomb graves like probing fingers, spilling century-old bone among the weeds; Comiski was roused by the odor of lye.

1

The gathering was sedate, almost elegiac. One of the policemen stood in the Johnson grass, swinging his club strung on braided leather; his partner sat on the edge of an open coffin, writing out his report. They ignored the ancient Negro sexton who cowered to one side, hat in his hands. The photographer, trussed by the straps of camera and light meter, dark moons of perspiration beneath the arms of his cord suit, turned on Comiski with what sounded like an accusation: "It's disgusting!"

The exposed cadaver was dressed in the style of the Dryades Street funeral parlors — sheer frock coat and striped trousers shredding like cheesecloth, moldy cardboard shoes; the stained wood of the coffin lid had disintegrated under pressure from a tire iron which lay abandoned in the weeds. Comiski peered inside the crypt at a pile of rubble laced with lye, marking the final resting place of the previous tenants; he turned over the headstone with one foot, recognized the name — PARKS. Not so much disgusting as forlorn: nothing to keep out the rot and the ghouls.

"You can make plenty out of this mess, Comiski," one of the cops said. "Ole Parks would have been mortified, seeing hisself exposed like that. One thing you could say about Parks; he kept hisself clean."

Comiski turned to the sexton. "What's become of the head?"

"Cain' say, Cap. I done tol' dese gent'mens, dey must'a took it 'long wid 'em."

"Voodoos, most likely." The cop grinned. "Voodoos 'n haints."

The photographer touched Comiski's arm. "We couldn't

run a picture of that. It's enough to make you spew."

"Shoot it," Comiski said, and he went to look for a telephone.

The red light announced that the short-wave radio was warming, attuning itself to the rush of information Comiski sought — complaints, misdemeanors, and, if all went well, atrocities. His hands trembled as he set the paper cup among the teletype copy littering his desk, raised the window instead of switching on the air conditioner. The November air — humid and still warmed by a declining tropical sun — offered him the odor of surgical spirit rising from the morgue, the smell of fatback frying in the prison kitchen, the sweet stench of a ton of hops stewing in the brewery across Broad Street. White cumulus hung in the sky; the metallic *chunk* of shuttled freight cars carried up from the railway yard; the drone of afternoon traffic was just beginning. Comiski could see the prisoners from the first tier lining up for early supper. In the courtyard below his window, the peach tree displayed furled and blighted leaves wrapped in cobweb — proof that it had survived another New Orleans summer.

Comiski sat down, sampled his coffee, began to cry. He hunched forward, straining the seams of his plastic raincoat, ignoring the short-wave that stuttered and shrieked; some part of his brain soaked up the patter, fed back the pertinent information like pabulum. He made no effort to wipe away the tears. The nights were getting shorter, the hangovers more intolerable: he always thought it would be the other way around. Autumn was the year's real beginning. He had greeted the last ten from the same position — straining the joints of his chair, savoring the blind man's coffee, clamping down at quitting time on the twisted end of a Marsh Wheeling cigar. In those years his ambitions hadn't changed; he looked forward to the track opening on Thanksgiving Day, a game of handball that evening, a drink to break up his walk home through the Quarter. The deviation bothered him: tears were the residue of bad dreams.

Comiski found solace in the familiar green walls about him, unpainted in that decade. The scuff marks at the foot of the couch tallied up the number of policemen who had used it to sleep off hangovers; the exposed hands of the Royal Crown Cola clock hanging above the police teletype machine had once again strangled on the wire. An open drawer in his desk was stuffed with copies of *Sports Illustrated;* old cracked handball gloves, and an empty cigar box. From where he sat Comiski could see the depression worn in the floor by the air conditioner's continuous drip. And there was the table, cigarette burns along the edges like stitching on an old quilt: it had supported an unreckonable number of newspapers, racing forms, card games that started on Fridays when he was leaving and were still going on when he returned on Monday mornings, whiskey and peanuts on Mardi Gras, a green plastic tree with synthetic snow turned gray on Christmas; and, once, six beefy cops with their trousers around their ankles, enjoying the ribald courtship of two aging hookers picked up on Decatur.

The table also reminded him of Parks. He used to sit there in the mornings before the first race, making his rapid calculations on the back of the form, throwing out elaborate jibes, courtly and successful — a survivor. Parks was the only Negro Comiski had ever known who could elicit civility from the ordinary policeman. He kept up a constant patter of amenities, and yet there was dignity in that lean hatchetlike profile — the shiny linen suit, the Knights of Columbus stickpin, never explained, the wingtipped ventilated shoes, and printed handkerchiefs. No one could ever spot Parks's racket: he didn't make book but could get a bet down on any sporting contest in the country within twenty minutes; he wasn't a bondsman but occasionally arranged bail and always seemed to prosper. He owned a horse, a pacer, enjoyed his day at the track.

Not anymore, Comiski thought. Since his death in a room off Basin Street, Parks was forgotten; the sight of the body that morning, the fusty suit and shoes, was unsettling. Crimes and criminals had a way of repeating themselves, and Comiski could accept the pranksters who left dead rats on trolley seats and stuck razor blades into the running boards of children's slides, but he drew the line at grave robbers.

Comiski vomited into the wastebasket, fouling his shoes; the telephone was ringing.

"Got anything on the Head?" asked Darrow.

"Nothing yet."

"What kind of an attitude is that, Comiski? Is this the Crusader speaking? Is this incentive?"

Comiski said decisively, "Screw you." In the background he could hear the assistant city editor singing, in a high falsetto, "I ain't got no *body*...."

"Sounds like you got a mouthful of red beans and rice this afternoon, my boy. You got any idea who disturbed that nigra's rest?"

"No, Darrow. It's not much of a story."

"Not the right attitude a-tall. The public deserves to know the truth and it is the truth we give them, because if you've read your new style book — which you haven't and won't — we are a modern newspaper."

"One of the last of the great metropolitan dailies."

"That's right," Darrow said. "Now you see if you can't hustle us up something. And I need a savory side-ball for the final. I feel like a good aggravated rape this afternoon, Comiski. How about you?"

''I'll work on it."

"You do that. And you have yourself a good game, you hear?"

Comiski replaced the receiver, wiped his mouth on his sleeve. He would never have believed, a few hours earlier, that he would have been physically capable of consuming a quart of beer and a mound of fried rice and shrimp. He gazed into the wastebasket, blamed his misery on rancid soy sauce. A Chinese conspiracy. They were trying to poison off vital members of the American press by luring them into Fong's. He tried to see the old Mandarin who owned the place as sinister: he barely had enough strength to discourage flies from alighting on his bald speckled head, often went to sleep propped against the cash register. Comiski couldn't deny that the man was inscrutable — a sure sign of Oriental subversion. Judging from Fong's clientele, they would be killing off considerably more whores than journalists.

Comiski opened the filing cabinet, located the file marked "Unusual/Unsolved Murders," took out a bottle of Jim Beam. He dashed the blind man's coffee grounds into the wastebasket, poured bourbon into the cup, and drank. Azam and azack:

6

light breaks where no sun shines. He was fortified for rape, whispered, "Then flash'd the living lightning from her eyes,/ And screams of horror rend th' affrighted skies..."

He couldn't remember the rest. After all the years, bits and pieces of poetry still insinuated themselves into his life; the fact that he had once intended to be a teacher — a professor of grammar and associated arcania — seemed grotesque. Comiski had taken a reporting job for a change, with no intention of staying; it was strange and mortifying how he sought out a slot for which he seemed least suited and then clung to that slot like a beleaguered crab. He tried to imagine himself being raped by an eight-foot black stud with gleaming red eyes, a chicken bone skewering one ear and a honed oyster opener clutched between his teeth; he came back to the thought of tears.

Comiski found the racing form in his desk, looked up the horse that had belonged to Parks. He remembered an underfed gray, mean eyes, a quick starter with no guts — Driven Snow. Out of habit he wrote down the jockey's name: it was the kind of lead he despised, a possibility that might relegate him to the identification bureau or the Clerk of Courts office for an hour, might even take him through the dim airless corridor of a downtown hotel looking for someone who wasn't there.

He took the slip of paper into the office next door. ID was a second home: the framed blowups of fingerprint prototypes, the rubber-topped tables where offenders were processed, the ink rollers, and the smell of strong soap were as familiar as the trappings of his own cubicle; he moved freely among the rows of files. In his sleep Comiski could conjure up the format of cards entombing murderers and pimps alike, reducing everyone to a pair of glaring photographs, blunt statistics, prints like the tracks of a wounded animal. The jockey's name surfaced; Comiski sucked on his unlit cigar, took down the information with short strokes of the pencil. There was enough to go on — the barest excuse for him to interrupt his routine, to hustle and earn some miserable overtime. In the beginning that lead would have meant the welcomed opportunity to dig someone out of a comer and learn something; now it just meant extra work.

Comiski was comfortable, didn't want to move. He looked again at the dying tree in the courtyard, the piles of grass cuttings, a rusted radiator: he remembered when it was a garden, cultivated by two aging warders who manicured the Peter's burr, raised a gawky banana tree in the far corner. One September a hurricane uprooted it and filled the courtyard with broken shingle. The morning after the storm Comiski found a strange wormlike creature clinging to his broken screen, realized it was a butterfly that had lost its wings in the storm; he tried to rescue it, to entice it with bits of sugared doughnut to come inside and recuperate. Somewhere he had read that butterflies only live for an hour or two after emerging from the cocoon, and during that time they fly wildly about searching for another butterfly with which to mate. Comiski wondered if his butterfly had managed to score. The glazed capsule eyes had told him nothing, reflected terror and amazement, the ugly tubular body and translucent legs clinging for life. Comiski had rushed down the hall to get a glass; when he returned, the butterfly was gone.

He began to count the autumns, grew confused. The fingerprints stared down at him like comatose eyes, at once accusing and indifferent; it occurred to Comiski to check for his own record, to search the files for a photograph of a stout balding man in a plastic raincoat, eyes averted. But he had never been arrested, never applied for a gun permit, had never been printed. I'm off the record, Comiski thought. I'm clean.

He left the building without returning to his office, hailed a cab from the front steps. Dirty roiled clouds were already gathering on the horizon; a muggy wind blew up Tulane Avenue, driving dust through the gutters, billowing Comiski's trouser legs. The facade of the Criminal Courts building overshadowed him — a fresco of Egyptians gathering grain; it faced the strip of bondsmen's offices, bars and used-car lots across the avenue, and he felt himself pursued, caught in a squeeze between the hustlers and the establishment.

Climbing into the cab, Comiski thought he remembered the dream — the tentative promise of early morning. It faded when he touched the worn upholstery, sensed the lingering presence of passengers who dribbled cigarette ashes and gum wrappers onto the floor. He looked toward the Claiborne Street housing project beyond the expressway, imagined the sun penetrating that wilderness. In the evenings he felt an almost tangible force begin to stir throughout the city — in tenement hallways, public lavatories, the bars along St. Charles that smelled of rancid port — gaining momentum with the darkness like fog moving in from the river, collecting in low places behind the docks, beneath overpasses, in deserted parks. Over the years the force had grown stronger: it was the sum total of every illegal act committed, and after keeping tally for so long, Comiski could feel it tugging at his ankles, knew the musty odor of evil like that of a blanket wrapped around a drowned man.

He got out of the cab abruptly in front of Charity Hospital and walked across to Larry and Katz. It was early: the place was empty except for an off-duty narcotics detective named Delaverne, but a group of black men stood on the pavement outside the window, buying their bottles over the sill. The bartender served them without speaking, raking the coins across the board, jabbing at the register. A long pine shelf to his right supported three .38-caliber revolvers, the bluing dulled by dust. The rough floorboards had never tasted wax, and the cuspidors were overflowing; yellowed photographs of dead or forgotten boxers covered one wall.

Comiski ordered a beer, began to beat the pockets of his raincoat as if he were on fire. He located the new handball, a knot of potential energy that would give him pleasure on the rebound, make him sweat; sweating was a cathartic and a kind of atonement for a body that had become, after thirty-seven years, cumbersome and slightly ludicrous. Comiski felt like a retired and dissipated athlete, erect but hindered by an encroaching gut; in spite of his strength, he was too docile on the handball court, shamed by breathlessness and the inundation of sweat that rendered his gym shorts transparent and coursed down thick white legs, soaking his canvas shoes. He might have been treading on sponges: his tracks left the polished floor treacherous.

Delaverne said, "You hear about that nigra, Parks?"

"I saw him. What there was left."

"What'll they think of next? It's disgusting."

"Mortifying," Comiski said.

"You know something?" Delaverne wiped his thick brindle

mustache with the back of his hand. "Parks was the only nigra I ever knew that didn't smell. You know, just a little bit."

Comiski drank. He thought he heard static coming from a hidden radio, the ringing of a distant telephone reaching out for him. His duties had become so stylized: a regimen of criminal code digits translated into a daily report, an impersonal summation of the more interesting transgressions. Comiski had done his bit for the day, shoveled the garbage into the chute so the hacks in the city room could cull through it. He knew from experience that Darrow would lead the story about Parks with a poem, something about death and mutability lifted from his tin box of eschatological verse scribbled on thumb-worn index cards.

Delaverne said, "You heard anything about the conspiracy?"

"Christ, not another one."

"It's not queers this time. It's supposed to be Nigras."

"Bullshit," he said solemnly.

"The word's out there are some funny ones in town."

"Not the average everyday ones?"

"The hired and paid revolutionary types."

"And who is it that hires and pays them?"

"That's an interesting question, Comiski. Could be the Commies, they're usually around somewhere."

"Yes, indeed. You could almost say the Commies are one of life's invariables."

"Now you're talking," Delaverne said.

Comiski resisted the urge to have a real drink. The array of whiskey bottles towered above him like glass stops in an enormous organ, each containing an orb of light — promises of love and happiness incubating merrily away. Thick negroid voices drifted in through the window like incantations, "No more'n a pint o' David. I got to git back to de chirren. No David? De Brothahs'll be jes fine."

Not now, Comiski reasoned, and he went outside.

He stood on the curb's edge and stared up at the glaring pink neon that asserted itself in mindless repetition. ANDKATZLARRYANDKATZLARRY. The transistorized voice of Ray Charles carried across the street from the lot where the Negroes sat on concrete blocks, drinking their wine; two blocks away, in the Charity emergency ward, a victim screamed — a sustained sexless outburst signifying neither pleasure nor pain.

Not now, but definitely later.

He was being hailed. An unmarked patrol car drove past; the lumpish face of one of a hundred policemen with whom he was acquainted called out, "Hey ya muthah, wheah ya at?"

Comiski took a threatening step forward, betrayed his confusion and his bad humor by shouting, "Shove it!" and demonstrating.

LITTLEBIT cowered behind the calico skirts of a stuffed mammie holding a tray of souvenir pralines. The lisping of big machines grew louder; there was no time to hide. He watched the motorcycles approach along Bourbon Street, cruise past the Old Absinth House, scattering tourists gripping pink hurricane glasses from Pat O'Brian's and a clot of admiring Tulane fraternity boys. The riders' helmets swiveled from side to side; Littlebit waited until he could read the plaque that rose from the fender of Bud's Harley like a chrome-plated dorsal fin — CRESCENT CITY CYCLISTS — then closed his eyes.

The machines labored past, the resonance of perforated

mufflers flooding the narrow street, swamping the competitive blares of ersatz Dixieland and hard rock and the patter of barkers flanking the strip clubs. They had missed him. He opened his eyes, clawed at the back of his thin pocked neck, watched the motorcycles pull up at the curb farther down the street. Bud and Grunt sauntered into Sloppy Joe's without bothering to remove their helmets, shouldering the pedestrians aside; Littlebit hesitated, darted across Bourbon and into the scented darkness of LaFite's in Exile'.

An oily Sicilian in a fedora and velveteen cutaway perched at the bar — a hustler from the penny arcade on Royal — his smile revealing carious teeth. Littlebit ignored him; he had things to think about — real problems. When they found him, they would punish and humiliate him, force him to drink, put the bitches on to him, maybe even lock him in the garage for a day, but they would never hurt him. Littlebit had his talent: he was useful.

His boots hung in midair, three inches short of the bar-stool rungs. The lingering jeweled fingers of the bartender served his glass of Pepsi; Littlebit looked up into his acquiescent lamp-tanned face — flesh stained by iodine — turned away with disdain. The eyes of the other patrons were on the newcomer, watching for his play, his preference; they were heavy trade for the most part — mean professional boys uninterested in people's problems.

Sex for Littlebit was secondary — a trial and an embarrassment. He often wanted to lie next to something warm and unaggressive, to feel the rhythm of another person's breathing and attempt to pace it. Such a simple state wasn't easy to obtain: even when he offered money, his partners became uneasy,

13

indignant. Only after the humiliating act did he experience brief respite and fulfillment, followed by mockery.

He took a dark orange capsule from the watch pocket of his Levi's, placed it on the back of his tongue, and washed it down with the Pepsi. The amphetamine would provide stamina, make him garrulous; he would need guts and a line of chatter, when they found him. After taking the capsules for two years — to bring him up out of sleep, for early morning workouts at the track — his kidneys complained. But Littlebit was easily surfeited, felt the old resentment: he was weary of the role of jockey and a runt's dilemma — the necessity of buying children's clothes, headiness in a single glass of beer, bad digestion, solitary nights, a lifetime of swaggering and bandy callused legs that dangled short of solid support.

The blast of an engine echoed along the street. He was acutely aware of the drink's carbonation, the drug's assault, and the sourness of his saliva: the things they were capable of doing. He remembered the moonscape of gravestones and the web of rusted iron filigree, heard whispered obscenities, recoiled from the cloying chemical odor. Littlebit had glimpsed maggots in the glare of the flashlight, writhing in the cloth like bits of iridescent thread; he was sure he understood the meaning of blasphemy. When Grunt thrust his hands into the gaping box, Littlebit experienced a new kind of fear — nothing was safe, ever. They had wrapped the thing in newspaper and stuffed it into the saddlebags, as if they were stowing beer for a ride to Biloxi.

He listened as the motorcycle pulled away and turned the corner toward Rampart, opened up with the clatter of cannon; that would be Bud, with his special cutouts designed to achieve

14

the maximum racket. Littlebit had heard somewhere that riding a big noisy machine could make a man impotent; he knew it would never happen to Bud — he seemed invincible.

Littlebit scratched at his neck. He wanted out: there were other towns, other tracks — he could always go home. He no longer cared about the money, wanted to be safe and away. Late one night he could pack his gear and slip across the Pontchartrain Causeway and into Mississippi. A vague sense of nostalgia came over him — people without faces, streets without names; he had come a long way since racking balls at Mandel's pool hall in Bay St. Louis.

He pinched himself, welcomed the pain. In the tinted mirror behind the bar he could see Grunt's reflection — faded Levi's, brass belt buckle encrusted with turquoise, a crumpled package of Picayunes rolled up inside one sleeve of his T-shirt; Grunt jostled the helmet under one arm like a severed head.

"My, my," he said, taking a stool. "You having yourself a time, Littlebit?"

"I'm doing all right."

Littlebit couldn't look at that face.

"Give me a Jax, Linda," Grunt told the bartender. He began to slowly roll his muscular shoulders. "You reckon that little fella over there knows how to French?"

"You better watch it," Littlebit snapped.

Grunt drank some of his beer, blew bubbles in the rest. The bartender slipped out onto the floor, leading with his elbows, and dropped a quarter into the juke box; a parody of Sophie Tucker relieved the silence.

"You shouldn't be running off," Grunt said. "Bud don't like it."

"I'm not married to Bud. Besides..." Littlebit's voice quavered. "Who's running?"

"Bud don't want you getting lost before opening day. We got to take care of you."

"What's that supposed to mean?"

Grunt drained his glass, brought it down hard against the bar. "Let's blow this place. We got a delivery to make."

Littlebit shuddered. "Jesus, no."

Grunt raised both arms, hiking up his shirt to reveal a hairy midriff marked with a swath of axle grease and the ugly linked edge of a three-foot length of chain wrapped carelessly about his waist, partially hidden beneath his belt.

"I'm action," he announced.

No one questioned the appraisal. The Sicilian tittered, kept his eyes riveted to the bottom of his glass; Grunt herded Littlebit out onto the pavement.

"Where's your bike?"

"At the pad. Fuel line's clogged."

Littlebit lied badly: he hated his motorcycle — a big Honda, which they derided as effete but which he found heavy and unmanageable, even threatening. Motorcycles were distasteful for the same reason horses were: he was afraid of their urgency, revolted by the excess of effort, the trembling and heavy breath — instruments of antagonism.

Dangling from the back fender of Grunt's machine was an aluminum plate stamped with the picture of an old soldier in a gray uniform, gripping a broken sword and the standard of a Confederate flag; beneath him was the inscription, FORGET, HELL! Grunt's saddlebag bulged with something unspeakable.

"Double up." Grunt kicked the engine off with a single stroke.

LITTLEBIT held on to the leather thong. His foot touched the saddlebag; he thought he was going to be sick. The motorcycle lunged away from the curb, and Bourbon became a wind tunnel, crowded with lights and fleeing figures. He knew what they might do to him, if they decided he was no longer useful; he wondered exactly how they would do it.

An overfed tabby with a broken tail streaked out from behind a parked car. Grunt made no alteration in course or in speed; the cat, realizing its mistake, stood staring in terrified indecision. Someone shouted. Littlebit looked back, glimpsed a man in glasses kneeling in the gutter. The cat's soft white belly was exposed; it thrust upward with one paw, as if pursuing a fly through a dream. Then it lay still.

Just like that, Littlebit decided.

BLINDING white lights reflected off the polished floor, giving the illusion of rising heat. The walls were cool and damp, sprinkled with the scuff marks of a thousand glancing balls — a fresco of dead leaves driven by the wind.

Comiski stood in the comer of the court like an unruly child; his sweat-soaked gym clothes hung like bandages, and a deep flush extended upward into the line of fine hair, making a beacon of his bald spot. He breathed shallowly, rapidly at first and then not at all. His heart raced on. He could feel it pounding against his ribs, could actually see its thrusts against the shirt — a small animal trying to escape from a soggy paper bag.

Comiski tendered the frantic organ, wanted to pray; to ask that his heart stop beating was suicide. The ludicrous aspect of his own death offended him.

LITTLEBIT fell among the burlap sacks stuffed with feathers, hit his head against a barrel full of oyster shells. Chicken fluff drifted across the mouth of the alley and into the angle of streetlight like wet sooty snow.

"Innards 'n fish heads," Hoppy scoffed. "The smell's enough to stunt yer growth."

Littlebit lived on the alley, was accustomed to the stench of the fish and poultry market next door.

"I keep the window shut, stupid," he said.

"Why yew little facker..."

"All right," Bud told them.

Littlebit worked his back up the wall until he was standing. The darkness hid his terror; if Hoppy hit him again, he wouldn't have to see it coming. Bud sucked on the final inch of his Camel; the coal glowed, lit up blunt clenched fingers, the hollow of one cheek. He seemed distracted, embroiled in smoke, gazing out into Magazine Street where Grunt waited, one boot resting on the gas tank of his machine. A man in a filthy overcoat crossed to the other pavement and moved past the darkened storefronts; Grunt watched until the man turned the corner and hurried toward the river. A barge horn moaned, laying claim to the channel; the night was beginning.

Bud said, "You know something I don't?"

"Not a thing, I swear."

"That nigger never said nothing?"

"No more than what I told you."

Bud sighed, scraped his boots among the gravel and broken glass. "We got to find that stuff," he said.

"Whatever you say."

"I don't want you running off again, you hear?"

"I hear you, Bud."

Littlebit felt tears gather in his eyes. It was easier than he had anticipated; he wanted to reach out and touch Bud's hand — a sign of thanks and admiration — but knew better.

Bud ground the cigarette out against the wall. "Next time," he said, "you'll be squirming."

"Amen," said Hoppy.

THE SHUDDERING eye of the St. Charles Avenue trolley swung around Lee Circle. Sparks flew from the overhead wire; the contraption ground to a halt with the shriek of steel punishing steel. Comiski, flushed and short of breath, swung aboard and took his seat among the last of the homeward-bound secretaries and coffee brokers. The carillon bells on top of the Hibernia Bank were completing a syncopated version of "Danny Boy"; the stuttering music touched a chord of memory — drinking bouts with forgotten buddies on the patio of the Napoleon House, trips by open car to Pass Christian, marriage. He tried to remember the words: *Oh, Danny Boy, the something something of something are waiting.* Or was it *falling?*

The trip uptown depressed him; the pattern was as familiar as the lurching machine in which he traveled — expectation, recrimination, anger, and, finally, loneliness. The routine was the only thing left of a brief and ridiculous marriage. It repeated itself without variation after eight or nine years, confined him to the downtown bars where he didn't have to see the spreading oaks, the irregular brick sidewalks and ghostly facades of the Garden District homes.

Comiski could barely remember a face. The pain always originated in his groin: she had long muscular legs, a vacuous smile cultivated in countless social engagements that appeared in the middle of their worst arguments, a habit of touching her teeth with the tip of her tongue when excited. He met her at a political rally; she was a debutante in search of a cause, and Comiski was a starting reporter fresh from the state university, full of confidence and irreverence. He accepted the fact that she wanted to come to his apartment, just as he later accepted marriage, his mother-in-law's hatred, his father-in-law's boozy attempts at camaraderie, his new wife's attempts to get into the bathroom each morning ahead of him, to apply a flawless mask of makeup. Comiski also accepted the necessity of stuffing himself into a tuxedo two or three times a year, to attend functions where his name and his bafflement offended people he had never seen before or since. When she left him — stepped into a cab and drove back up Prytania Street — it was as if his wife had simply spent a year at a foreign university and then decided to change her course of study.

Comiski put the blame on their apartment — a slaves' quarters on St. Anne where they seemed constantly on the point of collision. Their appetites coincided: they met head-on at the refrigerator, the radio, and the sink, in the narrow passage between the bed and the bookshelf, almost sat on one another's lap in the bathroom. They celebrated their first and last anniversary in that apartment; the thought still made him feel claustrophobic. Comiski could taste Jack Daniel's and fresh mint, charred game birds, could see his father-in-law's flushed face, buck teeth, and cowboy hat filling the doorway — his desperate enthusiasm — two Mason jars of mint julep under his arms. Behind him stood the immense black cook holding a platter piled with quail slaughtered on somebody's bean plantation, her crisp white uniform and paper cap like the vestments of a priestess, and behind her, grinning and resigned to a nightmare, was the chauffeur, already sweating in his wool uniform. The silver Chrysler nearly blocked the street: their entrance reminded Comiski of a circus act in which a procession of clowns unpacks itself from a baby carriage.

Comiski, his wife, and her father sat on the bed and drank from the Mason jars; the cook and the chauffeur confined themselves to what was supposed to be the kitchen — an alcove partitioned off by a curtain. Cigar smoke and steam filled the room. The pictures fell off the walls, and when the feast was finally ready — burned in the overheated oven and served on top of a suitcase covered with a bedspread — the three of them were drunk. Comiski's father-in-law launched into a benediction with bleary eyes and slack jaw, his voice assuming a biblical cadence: *Lawd God, bind these two young people in the etuhnal mantle of Thy muhcy — grant them, oh Lawd, the benefits...*

The chauffeur sat on a beer crate, tried to hide his head behind the curtain. He had taken off his jacket and rolled up his sleeves, revealing arms like the blades of dull butcher knives; one white eye peered at Comiski through the fringe, filled with wonder and amazement. The cook stood over them with the steaming birds, awkward and patient, eyes clamped shut in atonement for a world of sinners, her hands trembling with the platter's weight.

Lawd — LAWD — grant now in this Thine hou-wah of felicitay and endurin happiness all they muhcy, and let us not forget Thy bounty if the days do for a time grow dahk...

Comiski had no more vivid memory and no keepsakes,

just artifacts left over from the disastrous campaign. There was the couch — a wedding present from his wife's mother — that had stuck with him through the years like a dispirited but loyal beast, wounded by a thousand ashes, scorched once when he passed out with a cigar in his hand and it almost became his funeral pyre. There was the electric toaster he was constantly trying to repair with thick, unskilled fingers, and the straight razor — a family heirloom bestowed upon Comiski by his father-in-law with ceremony. The blue steel blade was inscribed with the names of his wife's grandfather and great-grandfather — whoremonger and slave-beater respectively, Comiski suspected; the mother-of-pearl handle was wrought to fit the hand and displayed, on the butt, two precise notches. *This blade has quieted down no less than two unruly black bucks...* He didn't believe the story, but sometimes when he was shaving his finger touched the notches, and he nicked himself.

Comiski had gone to fetch his wife after a week passed. His mother-in-law received him cordially; he sat in a lawn chair and took part in chatter about storm windows. Another goddamn hurricane. His father-in-law stood among the rosebushes, dressed in what he considered to be work clothes — riding boots and a sport shirt with the sleeves rolled up — shouting orders at the chauffeur. The air was motionless, expectant: there wasn't a bird in sight, and the rattle of ice cubes in Comiski's glass was deafening. He knew something was wrong, felt a wash of desolation like the impact of those waves laden with flotsam that rose up out of the shallows off Grand Isle, where they spent their honeymoon. He wanted to raise his arm and shield himself from the vision of that dark stretch of sand, the off-shore oil derricks — skeletal fins of fornicating sea monsters — the clouds of mosquitoes droning among the cypress, the heat and the ooze of that timeless unnatural land. *And where, madame, is your daughter?* He couldn't forget the dewy curls pressed against the woman's head, the thin painted lips out of a low-budget horror film, her words delivered with the sanctity and the finality of a papal bull, "I'm happy to say she is at this moment riding a bicycle through Provence."

Comiski clambered down from the trolley at the corner of Jackson Avenue, stood on the corner looking up and down St. Charles. His reason for being there was obscure. A score of Lucky Dog salesmen pushed their wares out of a garage across from the Pontchartrain Hotel, wearing striped jackets and cardboard hats, fanned out to hawk a taste of deprivation along with the low quality wieners, stale buns, and watery mustard trundled about in carts made to resemble huge hotdogs on wheels. They reminded Comiski of the wine-sodden floor of the Cave Inn, stalking through the streets like scepters of his own conscience, and he bought a Lucky Dog as much out of a sense of atonement as hunger. He ate hunched over a trash bin on the corner, followed his supper with a drink in the Cameo, then headed toward the river.

The Irish Channel always held something for Comiski: he picked up on the debris — the rats peering through the grates, the smell of bad oysters, graffiti covering the posted bills. The professional eye. Darrow once told Comiski that he was their best man for peeping over the partitions in the men's lavatories, for thumping the kernels out of the upchuck. News mogul of the first water.

The house was an old mansion converted into a warren, with a view of trash blown against the iron gate and the distant girdered belly of the bridge strung on cold blue lights. The woman who answered the door hung back in the shadows, one arm across her stomach as if cradling a tumor; she said, "Yeah?"

Comiski knew his role. "Morton around?" he asked.

"No, he ain't. What is it?"

"Business." He winked.

"Morton," she said. "That's good. They call him Littlebit. You from the track?"

"That's right."

"I'd imagine he's down at Mary's. With them others. You see him, you tell him he owes me."

Comiski thanked her, moved on.

The sign was visible from the steps, an unadorned board stating the problem without the benefit of neon lights — Mary's Tavern. A brace of motorcycles stood outside in the street, tilted in unison like a gate of horses waiting for the bell, chrome pipes and leather resplendent in the headlights of passing cars. The sound of electric guitars spilled through the open door.

He loosened his tie, made his entrance. The narrow room was crowded and filled with smoke; Comiski saw three men in black denim and leather standing at the center of the bar. He took a stool next to them, ignoring the silent rebuke of the bouncer sprawled at the far end, and ordered bourbon and a glass of beer.

"Make it, Fats. That pew's took."

He had just thrown back the bourbon and wanted to chase it with beer, knew if he did he might have to pick splinters of glass out of his gums. He smiled, resented the fact that he was always being caught off balance: his wife asked him to open the cab door, and he did it out of plodding good manners, not realizing that he might not have opened it; Darrow always got the knife in. They were tripping him up.

Comiski swallowed, pushed his ear in the direction of that petulant voice; it instructed him, "Move your ass!" He obeyed, took out a handkerchief and wiped the seat of the stool, then drank off the beer in grateful swallows.

"If it ain't Jackie Gleason," the little man said. "We got us a personality here, Hoppy."

Comiski found another little man at his elbow wearing a red bandanna and needle-nosed cowboy boots. Hoppy's freckles, colorless lashes, and chipped teeth gave him an air of dissolute adolescence; coarse red hair buoyed up the gold-plate cross on his chest, covered the backs of his hands like pig bristles, festooned the rhinestone snaps on his cuffs.

"Yew ought to be ashamed of yewerself, Dude," Hoppy told him. "What would a big ole fellar like yew want to bother Littlebit about? Hit's just foolish, making trouble for yewerself like that."

"Trouble is for others," Comiski philosophized; he told the barmaid to give them a round.

"Take your beer and stuff it," Littlebit said, clawing at the sores on his neck. "You tell him, Hoppy."

"Now just a little minute. I take that as a rite kindly offer the dude is making." He spoke with an up country twang that never got west of Texarkana. "Littlebit here don't much like to drink. Hit ain't really that he don't like hit, but hit gives him them little biddy bubbles. But yew take Grunt — often as not he drinks so much beer hit likes to make him drunk."

25

The music rose to a crescendo, died in a jangling cacophony as if someone had pulled out the plug. Grunt stepped forward, accepted Comiski's hospitality in silence, drank off one glass of beer and then another.

"Yew see what I mean, Dude?" Hoppy said. "Now he wants anoth'ern — just like a billy goat eating turnips. Look here, Bud."

A fourth man came from the dance floor, parting the crowd like a wedge; a big-breasted girl with hair gone orange at the roots followed him, broke away at the periphery of the circle. Bud's cyclist's cap was encrusted with medallions, held in place by a greasy leather thong. His face was lopsided, with a depression where one cheekbone should have been; his speckled yellow eyes never seemed to blink.

Littlebit shrilled, "He sat on your stool, Bud!"

"Well, now he's off it."

Comiski refused to be dismissed; he ordered another round and stepped aside with his whiskey so Grunt could line the glasses up along the bar and drink them off. That virtuoso performance, Comiski decided, was going to appear on his expense account. The band started up again; farther along the bar a stool toppled and glass shattered. The barmaid set more beers before them, said to no one in particular, "We're gonna have ourselves a butt-grabbin' good time," and began to dance.

Comiski felt Hoppy grip his elbow. Grunt's stupid good-natured face was inches from his own; he studied the old scar tissue and tufts of eyebrow — the only tribute to what probably amounted to a quarter of his life spent sparring with faster welterweights in Curley's Gym — smelled his surfeit of beer.

26

"You and Myrt show us how," Grunt said. "Go on, she's just dying."

Comiski turned up his palms like a minstrel, felt a thumb in his kidney, shuffled along behind the girl with the heavy breasts. On the dance floor couples jostled each other with constrained fury; Comiski struck the classic pose, moved his partner through a series of ponderous two-steps. He wondered what she would say if he told her he had danced at the finest Mardi Gras balls. Would you believe these feet have tripped the light fantastic beneath the very eyes of Rex? The girl kept her face averted, passive in her humiliation; he felt sorry for her and for himself, was thankful when the singer began to mouth the microphone, giving them an excuse to move back to the bar.

Comiski was offered a stool; he ordered another round, took the barmaid's hand when she brought him change.

"Don't worry," he told her. "My wife's bicycling through the south of France."

"No shit?"

"None whatever. Right now she's eating Camembert, drinking Chateau Rothschild, flinging her body into the wine-dark sea. Her legs have become so strong from riding that bicycle that she crushes her Latin lovers and is doomed to a lifetime of coitus interruptus."

"Watch your mouth, you!"

Comiski looked into the mirror behind the bar, found that his mouth contained an unlit cigar. His dancing partner began to cuddle him; he didn't resist as her hands probed his armpits, caressed his gut, felt along the edge of his belt in their search for the pistol butt, the handcuffs' chain, the leather case containing a badge. The hands encountered nothing but Comiski's damp self; satisfied, the girl unzipped his trousers and sauntered back toward the dance floor.

He tried to laugh, fumbled with his flies. Bud and Grunt each took one of his arms and propelled him in the direction of the men's room, forcing him to hobble with his legs together; Comiski saw the bouncer moving off toward a disturbance behind the bandstand. He clawed at the rope handle on the door, felt it break as Bud wrenched him off balance by the lapel of his raincoat and Grunt pushed him from behind, as if Comiski were a cow being shoved into the slaughter chute.

Bud shut the door and leaned against it; Grunt leapt the stream that dribbled from a corner of the clogged urinal and turned to face him, one hand slipping inside his jacket. Comiski was more frightened by the audacity of his tormentors than by his impending death. He would kick Grunt squarely in the groin — an academic gesture of defiance. He prayed that when they finished stabbing him, he would fall away from the urinal.

Grunt was laughing. He held up a twisted homemade cigarette, gazed at it with comic crossed eyes, put it into his mouth and pretended to swallow, withdrew it again like a conjurer. Comiski's savior: grass. Give us this day our daily cannabis. He watched Grunt light it and inhale; Comiski was so relieved that he didn't protest when his turn came, took a mouthful of sweet smoke and, in his confusion, swallowed it. He had often watched the narcotics men practice the false inhale, had wondered if it was possible to keep the stuff out of the blood stream, found that it wasn't.

He declined another drag, watched Grunt caress the charred roach and stow it in his sock. Going out, Grunt whispered,

"For you, Dude. Just for you."

Comiski regained his stool, found himself ignored.

"I gunned ole Rastus five times out on the Lakefront," Hoppy was saying. "I knew that ole mail-order fan weren't no good, 'cause there weren't nuthin' in the paper. I chunked that fan up on the closet shelf and that last'un shot off and hit the mirror and didn't even bust hit..."

"Hey, Fats, I want another beer."

Three full glasses already stood before Littlebit in a puddle of perspiration; he stared at them, fondling the back of his neck.

"So you're a jockey," Comiski said.

"Who says? Nobody said nothing about jockies. Who the hell are you?"

"I thought I heard..." He raised his hands, grinning like an idiot; Bud was standing beside him. "What's your line, friend?" Comiski asked.

"Sheet metal. What about you?"

Comiski resisted the urge to fashion himself into a real estate agent or an insurance salesman. Play it straight, he thought — disarm them with the truth.

"I'm a newspaperman."

Bud's eyes registered nothing. He thought he hadn't spoken loud enough, was about to repeat himself when he felt a wave of beer break against his leg, heard the smashing of glass about his feet and Littlebit's hysterical shouting.

"Bud, get this goddamn sonofabitch..."

Grunt and Bud hustled Littlebit across the room; Hoppy put his hand on Comiski's shoulder.

"Newspaper-man," he said meaningfully. "Listen here,

Dude, I used to do stunts for Wawerner Brothers, and I got this pitchur of me in my rig. I want yew to put hit in yer paper. Yew can say how my momma said I was born on a horse and jumped off hit onto a machine."

Comiski felt the beer seeping into his cordovans: he was clumsy, unacceptable in any type of society, immeasurably old. The edge of self-pity cut across his brooding, heralding the arrival of a state of drunkenness over which he had no control — the sniveling reprobate who astounded and disgusted him.

"Saddlin' up," Hoppy drawled. "We're making The Flame, if yew want to double."

Comiski knew better: the croaking voice of professionalism told him to cool it, call a cab, and hold on to the bar until it arrived. But anything seemed better than standing alone in a puddle of beer, exposed to the barmaid's hostility, the music's unflagging tug toward insanity, his own reflection; Comiski lunged outside.

The electronic din was replaced by the symphony of big machines warming up; the night was full of the smell of motor oil. Comiski was pulled down behind Hoppy, his feet fitted into actual riding stirrups. The others set out like a squad of futuristic warriors headed into the gloom of chemical warfare, helmets clamped in place, the luminous purple taillights converging in the darkness.

The wad of steel between Comiski's feet picked him up and thrust him into the wind; his face was numb, his ears ringing. The line of machines turned at the corner of Jackson and opened up with the clatter of gunfire; Hoppy accelerated straight across the intersection, defying the stoplight and the bus — a bright building on wheels — that slid to a halt with the blare of a horn. Hoppy's wrist dipped again; his stomach was hard beneath Comiski's hands. Beneath the visor Comiski could see the set of his jaw and a trace of red stubble. He shouted but heard nothing, pressed his cheek against the back of Hoppy's jacket; in a furniture store window he glimpsed his own bloodless face, a plastic raincoat whipped by the wind.

When Comiski opened his eyes again the smell of dust and oyster shells filled his nostrils; he saw the long shadow of the railroad embankment ahead, the warning crossed boards framed against the sky. With a shudder they cleared the tracks; it occurred to him — after the machine set down in the broken shale, trailing Hoppy's rodeo whoop — that they had been flying. The wharf was strewn with blocks for stacking cargo, and Hoppy maneuvered among them, swerved at the edge of the dock so that they seemed to hang out over the waters of the Mississippi that shone yellow in the light of the single moored tanker.

Comiski sank to his knees, spread his hands over the solid scuffed surface of planking. The motorcycle murmured; Hoppy pushed up his visor, lit a cigarette.

"Yew git yewerself on home, Dude," he said, "before yew git into trouble."

He drove slowly off, navigating among the blocks with one hand and smoking with the other. The taillights dropped out of sight; with the sound of distant thunder he was gone.

For a long time Comiski didn't move: like a praying man, he waited for inspiration.

LITTLEBIT watched the girl get up from the floor and begin to dress. The ritual fascinated him: women's flesh was

31

unmanageable, had to be shorn up and molded, and once the support was gone it spread everywhere, heavy and revolting. She sheathed naked thighs and haunches in bleach-spotted denim with a hip motion that only a woman could be guilty of, zipped up with difficulty, leaned forward and scooped her swinging breasts into an apparatus that reminded Littlebit of a horse feeder.

She went over to the bed — Littlebit's bed — and jostled the girl who lay between two masses of insensate male flesh that was Grunt and Hoppy; the girl woke up with wide staring eyes, and the first girl covered her mouth with her hand, waited for the terror to pass, helped her up. The two of them pampered their hair, conferring in hushed voices. This girl was hard and wiry; one nipple was larger than the other. The light blue lace edging her panties was torn; the sharp angle of her hipbone was stamped with a lavender bruise.

Littlebit turned away, waited for them to be gone. The room smelled of beer and stale cigarette smoke; the floor was littered with butts and crumbs from the feast of sardines and crackers eaten a few hours before. He slept badly in the chair, the darkness charged with jokes and the resonance of heavy breathing. A three-ring circus with the lights out. The scene sickened him; he felt tainted, as if the residue of communal sex had rubbed off on him. During the early morning hours he had gone to sit next to Bud — when he wasn't occupied — hoping that their hands might touch; when they did touch, Bud didn't draw his away immediately, waited until he wanted another cigarette. In the blaze of the match Bud's face looked strangely beautiful, in spite of the crushed cartilage. Littlebit was moved by pity, wished they had met under other circumstances; he let his mind drift, after Bud moved off toward the bed, through the fantasies of what might have been.

The girls went out. He waited until their footsteps reached the end of the hall, then went over to the washbasin. Bud lay on the floor, wrapped in the blanket, his head resting on a pile of dirty laundry and one arm across his eyes. He seemed to be sleeping, but you could never tell for sure: he might have been hiding the scars of the crash — when he hit a cow doing ninety and spent three months in the Galveston Veterans Hospital. Bud didn't like to be reminded that he hit a cow; everyone knew the story.

Littlebit took an amphetamine capsule out of the aspirin bottle, bent over the faucet, and washed it down.

"Pretty early to be turning on," Bud said.

Littlebit wheeled on him. "Who's turning on? I have to take these for my complexion."

"Sure you do."

Bud groped among the soiled towels and socks stiff as cardboard for his Camels; he carefully inserted a cigarette between his lips and lit it.

"Stinks in here," he said.

"Stinks outside, too."

"Some pad. How the hell do you breathe?"

Littlebit didn't want to fight, not while the others were asleep and he had Bud to himself; he turned his back on that white, athletic body.

"Want me to fry you an egg?"

"I don't mind."

"Real butter, Bud. Unsalted butter."

"That a fact?"

Bud began to cough — a hacking that reminded Littlebit that everyone was vulnerable. He took his folding army skillet from the shelf, wiped it out with newspaper, retrieved the butter and eggs from the outside sill, and slammed the window. He wished he had milk and flour and molasses, so he could show what he could do on a hot plate.

"Why'd that wag come looking for you?" Bud asked.

Littlebit faltered: it wasn't fair, starting in so early.

"I never saw him before. You know newspaper reporters, Bud — always nosing around. You shouldn't have let Grunt bust up that grave..."

"I don't want that fat-ass sparking the fuzz. We got trouble enough."

The butter boiled in the pan, turned dark and brackish; Littlebit broke the egg with one hand, turned to see if Bud had noticed his expertise. But he was staring at the hot end of his cigarette, his Levi's hanging open and his jacket draping his shoulders; smoke trailed from both nostrils.

"You reckon maybe that nigger's girl friend's got the stuff?" he asked.

"I got no idea. I never took any interest until you..."

"You worked for him, Littlebit. You rode a nigger's horse."

"And that's all I did. I don't know anything about any connection."

He turned the egg with a table knife, breaking the yolk.

"I'm sorry about that."

"I don't mind," Bud said.

Grunt and Hoppy stirred among the sheets, roused by the smell of cooking; they scowled in their sleep, rubbed their stubble-blighted chins together.

Bud began to wash. Something heavy and metallic rattled loudly in the basin; Littlebit turned in time to see him shove the shiny automatic pistol back inside his jacket.

"We got to find the girl," Bud said, and he went on washing.

Hoppy sat up, grinning and rubbing his eyes. He was stark naked except for the cross dangling from his neck; he sang with a husky nasal whine, *"Ain't hit fine, fackin on corn silks..."*

Smoke billowed up from the pan. Littlebit raised the window; his hand trembled as he dumped the burned egg into the alley.

THE POLICEMAN recalled some conflict, groped for his revolver, snored on. A plainclothes detective pulled a trolley past the door laden with suitcases and a television set — evidence bound for the courtroom; down the hall, a prison trusty whistled plaintively and with skill.

Comiski heard the short-wave crackling to life, bolted from the office. He was almost running when he reached the door leading down to the morgue.

"Hail mighty Charon," he said. "I seek admittance to the depths and converse with the shades."

The woman at the reception desk looked up from her confessions magazine, confused and resentful; he started down the steps, and the smell was at him. It boggled his senses: medicinal, nauseating, redolent of things decayed and forgotten, clinging to his clothes, bringing tears to his eyes. After years of chasing down auto fatalities and spotting gunshot wounds, Comiski hadn't grown accustomed to it; the smell of anisette, after-shave lotion, the solution used to clean the rest rooms at the track all reminded him of that subterranean white tiled room, the wall of steel refrigerators, the pallor of corpses like old gray rubber, the swinging doors worn by the passage of stretchers through which he made his entrance.

A stooped figure in a surgical apron sat hunched over a steel tray, working with a long crooked needle; he turned and squinted at Comiski. One lens of his spectacles was covered with a patch, like a drawn shade.

"A gentleman of the press," he whispered.

The body on the tray had two incisions running from the shoulders to the solar plexus and a single gash to the groin, bound with welts of heavy stitching. Comiski almost nodded in response to the cadaver's arm locked in a salutory gesture by rigor mortis; Gomer placed his po'boy sandwich on the edge of the tray, and Comiski couldn't suppress a shudder.

"What brings you down?" Gomer asked.

"I was wondering about old Parks. That business at the graveyard. Have you heard anything?"

"We don't hear much down here."

Gomer turned to the driver of the coroner's wagon who stood leaning against the refrigerators, in full view of his handiwork. The shabby uniform did not conceal the fact that his arms were abnormally short; his grin revealed unhealthy gums and total incomprehension.

"Coronary, wasn't it?" Comiski said.

"Believe so. He was a real stinker — plumb full of corn bread."

Gomer walked slowly across to his desk, opened a leather-bound notebook and thumbed through it, tossed it aside and opened another; he tilted his head from side to side, like a metronome.

"Coronary. It's all down here."

They were the most conclusive records Comiski ever read: the final entry in florid script, magenta ink.

"You didn't notice anything, did you? Anything suspicious."

Gomer's laugh was dry, insulted.

"We don't have suspicions down here, Comiski, only facts. That's what we're for."

"All right, damn it. Why would somebody steal an old man's head?"

"Don't need a reason," Gomer whispered. "It was niggers, wasn't it?"

Comiski didn't answer. He went back through the swinging doors and up the stairs; at the top he paused to catch his breath, found that Gomer's voice was still with him. It was a uniquely southern intonation — a man on the edge of panic, placated by the humiliation of what was nearest and most vulnerable — a voice that lurked in the conversation of almost every man Comiski knew. The sound of it conjured up the worst aspects of his surroundings. He remembered the smell of sweat and urine in the basement of the Parish Prison, ten years before, high beams clotted with cobwebs and the cornucopias of mud built by wasps, rusted iron rings driven into the walls where unruly Negro prisoners were beaten by an aging warder known as the Butcher. Comiski heard stories of him shrieking in the midst of as many as six dangling men, laying about him with lengths of hose, knotted rawhide, broken mop handles, locked in a frenzy of punishment and what he believed to be divine retribution that eventually killed him of exhaustion. The iron rings were still there, worn thin at the studs.

It must have been Gomer's voice that breathed into his

37

drunken brain, the night before, the recollection of a pair of black wizened ears bobbing in a jar of alcohol, set in the window of the barbershop in the town where he grew up. Comiski woke up that morning trailing the nimbus of several nightmares, but plagued in particular by the memory of a black man dying. He saw his uncles girding their loins as if they were going off to war, hitching up hunting breeches with red suspenders, strapping on revolvers and skinning knives and flashlights; there was an argument over dogs, as they loaded them into the pickup truck in the barnyard. Their bickering was laced with hysteria. Comiski was used to the excitement of hunting — a controlled violence — and the fact that the adults were hunting a man this time was natural enough. He knew Negroes to be working things, occasionally amusing companions, often objects of ridicule and unreasoning malice that he didn't understand but accepted: they were a sort of third sex that had nothing in common with his own fair origins and aspirations. Comiski was in grade school before he realized that a Negro could bleed.

There was no blood; he saw a charred unrecognizable carcass trussed with clothesline and dragged patiently behind one of the pickups, past a group of shacks lining an unpaved road where not one single shade was drawn to view the quarry. Hanging, burning, dismemberment, preservation: an arcane ritual more curious than horrible.

Comiski bypassed his office, went outside and hailed a cab from the steps. The Cajun driver complained bitterly about federal welfare programs; Comiski tuned him out, tried to think of ways of overcoming an intolerable environment. Sex, drink, religion, art, in that order. The static from the cab radio distracted him. Drops of rain exploded amid the soot on the windshield as the brief afternoon shower began. People on the sidewalks barely altered their pace, might not have noticed the rain — a tropical quotidian. Beyond the phallic thrust of the Trade Mart a rent in the clouds filled with a soft lavender glow, an intimation of the sun's parabola.

Light breaks, he thought. It does.

You seen some things, Mistah Comiski. You could make this bunch of white trash poh-lease hop.

The rain stopped as suddenly as it began; he got out at old Congo Square and walked. The building he sought was on the edge of Storyville, spawning ground of Dixieland and voodoo and other amenities of the Big Easy. The district attorney had driven most of the whores and the pushers out into the suburbs; real estate agents moved in, converting brothels into honeycombs of apartments for airline pilots and engineers from Michoud — the parvenues and new burghers who were changing the Quarter forever.

Parks's building had remained untainted. It leaned against the one next door like an aging reveler, the whitewash a thin skin of memory over warped boards; beneath the roof's overhang was stacked furniture — bedstead, a gutted couch, a refrigerator. Comiski stood on the doorstep and peered down the long empty hallway, wondered which was Parks's room.

He heard whispering to his left. Three white people — a bearded man and two women — sat among the upturned chair legs like fledgling sparrows forsaken in a nest, watching him. The man had the slack jaw and palsied stare of a syphilitic; the young woman's hair was bobbed short like a religious fanatic's. The older woman — thin, gray, and aggressive —

39

approached Comiski.

"We won't wait forever!" she cried.

"No, of course not."

"It's disgraceful. Novak's got us over a barrel — he hurts! But we ain't moving. Novak said he wants us to die. You got the check?"

Comiski understood. "I'm not from welfare," he said.

She barked at him, turned to the younger woman who squealed in response, exposing teeth covered with green scum. The woman turned back to Comiski. "Novak don't give us no rest — he wants us to die." Then she said, with absolute conviction, "Novak would cut off his mother's balls!"

He wanted to ask who this Novak was, but the woman went scurrying back to the others; they sat rocking on their haunches, staring through the forest of chair legs. A young cop ambled down the opposite sidewalk, marking car tires with a piece of chalk attached to a stick; he looked up and grinned.

"You must be Novak," Comiski said, crossing over. He remembered the name from the Seventh District rolls, had once heard him testify, recalling the details of a petty crime with self-assurance that the prosecution courted. Novak had a broken nose and his flat gray eyes were set too close together.

"I know you," he said. "How'd you like my animal act over there, Comiski?"

"What's going on?"

"Some nigger was paying their rent, but now he's dead and me and some of the boys had to put them out. You wouldna believed it — ten cats and they never opened the door on 'em. The smell! I mean we was skating on cat shit."

Comiski shrank from the whole scene; he couldn't help

40

wondering — it was a kind of caring — why Parks had paid the rent for three white deficients.

"She said something about a check."

"Welfare." Novak shook his head. "On days they got the coins, they drink a dozen pops apiece. Then they attack other tenants — spitting, like that. And then the son there's banging the mother and the sister. Now that ain't healthy, Comiski."

His head filled with a sustained shriek. Whether it was a car taking the corner, a woman being throttled, or an invention of his own sensibilities, he couldn't tell; Comiski felt the cogs of his mind beat a galloping retreat.

"The judge wants them in Mandeville," Novak went on, gesturing toward heaven with the chalk marker. "But we can't find nobody to sign the order. What we need is an unaffected party — we need you, Comiski."

Too far, my friend, Comiski thought. He hated the cop, illogically and without reservation, decided that Novak would never, regardless of his distinctions, receive his vote for Patrolman of the Week.

"I don't sign people away into asylums, Officer. But maybe we could run a little story on them — that might help rouse some interest."

Comiski started for the grocery store on the corner. Novak called after him, "First name's Gene! Eugene M. Novak."

Comiski telephoned the city desk, told the story straight, steeled himself: Darrow's cawing didn't touch him.

While he was talking, Comiski thought he heard the sound of motorcycles — a nightmare's resonance — but when he stepped outside again, the street was empty, glistening after the shower and coursed by oily rivulets of rainwater and grime marching together down toward the drain.

* * *

DELAVERNE found the clatter of gunfire reassuring. He closed his left eye, exhaled, squeezed off the final round; the revolver pumped his hand — a dependable response — and he noted another perforation in the target's smallest circle of white, edging dead center. Not bad with only three inches of barrel. He placed his Smith and Wesson on the podium, waited for the others to finish.

The line of deputies stretched away to his right — paunchy court warders unused to the firing line; the old man next to Delaverne jerked violently with each shot, as if he were flinging the bullets out with wrist action alone. His target remained untouched. Delaverne wondered if there might be someone out there in the swamp, beyond the hunter, menaced by the slugs that went screaming off through the Spanish moss. The acrid smell of burning cordite reminded him that hunting season was beginning.

The volley ended raggedly; the instructor raised both hands and called, "All arms down, advance and score."

Delaverne stepped out, flanked by Bates of the Vice Squad on his left, the only other competent marksman on the range; together they ringed their strikes with a grease pencil, tallied up on the edge of the target.

"You're five up on me," Bates said. "You must have been popping off at rats out at the dump."

"I like to keep my hand in. You never know, with these dope heads."

"My side of the sheet's as bad. You wouldn't believe what

queers come up with nowadays, Verne. Used to be you could slap a queen up-side the head and he'd confess all over you. Now you ask him real nice to come on out of that toilet stall, and he tries to burn you with his butane lighter."

"The chief's got a good idea," Delaverne said, "requiring all the men to shoot."

Bates agreed. "You never know."

They moved back to the firing line; Bates motioned him toward the benches beneath the awning.

"Let's take a smoke, before one of these old bastards plugs us."

Reluctantly, Delaverne followed. He wasn't in the mood for an argument — or a friendly discussion; he was experiencing the malaise that had lately begun to affect his afternoons. At the end of a day's work, a man deserved relaxation and freedom from care. Hunting would provide the freedom — long weekends away from the courts and his basement office, a respite from his wife's moroseness and the childless silences of their house, something to occupy his thoughts in the afternoons.

Mornings were the best: strong chicory coffee, banter with the men, a drink before lunch. After that things became grim, priorities obscure. Should he concentrate on the Quarter, busting the white freaks and the pushers? Should he step up efforts in the colleges, in spite of bad publicity? Or should he keep the real pressure on the black community, where narcotics seemed to flow in the streets and the big money passed hands? Delaverne wondered what Negroes found to do with all that money; the thought made him feel uneasy. He always kept the screws down in the Black Belt, passed the word to shoot if threatened: more than one pusher had been blown up in the last six months. Delaveme knew, at that moment, the trading in the projects was fierce.

Bates sat heavily, wiped his mouth with the back of his hairy fist, offered the package of cigarettes with an abrupt gesture that seemed rehearsed, conveying a sense of determination. Delaverne lit both their cigarettes; they stared out at the trees swamped in evening shadow. "When you coming over?" Bates asked.

"Coming over where?"

"With the boys. When are you joining up?"

"I already belong to an organization," Delaveme said. "The Fraternal Order of Police."

Bates blew a row of perfect smoke rings, picked a bit of tobacco from his tongue and inspected it.

"You'd be surprised to hear who's joined, Verne."

"I don't want to hear. I don't need that kind of trouble."

"Top men in the department care about what's happening to this country, just like your average patrolman. We all care, and so do you."

"It's against regulations."

Bates turned on him. "Somebody's got to take a stand. What about all the niggers?"

"I don't know," Delaverne admitted.

"What about all the Commies and Jews and students and freaks? What about the kooks taking over?"

"That's not much of an argument. You've got to have facts."

Delaverne's defense was selfish. Anyone could see there was a breakdown in many of society's institutions: a pervading permissive attitude made his own job too difficult, over-exacting, encouraged people to take the law into their own hands. He had been a policeman for fourteen years, and he looked forward to an early retirement and a small pension — he was planning to open a sporting goods store in the new shopping center on the West Bank. He might even take an occasional party back into the bayous he knew so well, to shoot teal and mallards — the well-heeled Texas financiers who had vague connections with the department. Delaverne could see himself in the role of guide without any loss of dignity: he had proven himself to be a man and a good administrator. Baptism by fire, the chief told him. An asset to the department.

"No time to be picky," Bates was saying. "The call's out, and if we don't answer, we'll be the ones taking the consequences."

"What do you reckon the consequences are?"

Delaverne wanted to know. It was possible that Bates and the others had access to classified information, specific facts; there was always another rumor about a conspiracy.

"You see the consequences all around you," Bates said. "A Commie for a federal judge, a nigger for a ward president, a Jew in the White House."

"No Jew in theWhite House."

"You just give them time." Bates pinched the cigarette butt as if it were an insect. "Let me ask you a few questions, Verne. No mikes out here. Now I want you to tell me how many nigger lawyers they got working for the Civil Liberties."

"I couldn't say."

"No less than two. Two niggers right in there with the rest of the kooks. Now tell me this — who's head of the Metropolitan Crime Commission?"

Delaverne thought for a moment. "A Jew," he said.

Bates nodded his head meaningfully.

"Were not just talking about the mess on the national level. We're talking about southern Louisiana and the parish of Orleans — were talking about *home,* Verne!"

A round of gunfire interrupted him. Delaverne couldn't deny the truth of what he was saying: there were some very strange things going on — ominous things. The turmoil, the freaks that he observed daily in the streets and on television made him reluctant to leave the protection of the police department. Delaverne wasn't sure who was behind the trouble — the new audacity — but whoever they were, they should pay. The night before he had been awakened by the sound of someone running across his front porch; he sat in his pajamas for an hour beside the screen door, his automatic twelve-gauge Remington across his knees, waiting for the shadowy figure to return. A feeling of uneasiness — a nameless threat — was affecting his life, tainting his afternoons, spoiling his modest ambitions: someone surely should pay.

"Who gets the welfare and the handouts and don't pay shit for taxes?" Bates asked.

"The Nigras, I suppose." Delaveme knew the chief never used the word *nigger.*

"Who commits most of the felonies and gets let off in court?"

"The Nigras."

"Who is it that's trying to take over on the national and on the local level, crime-wise and politics-wise?"

"The same."

"And who is it," Bates asked with satisfaction, "that tries to cut your throat and rape your wife every time you-all try to take a walk? That is if you want to take a walk. And at the same time who is it that has a right by law to move right on into your house?"

"The goddamn niggers," Delaverne said.

"The call's out, Verne. A new day's coming, and when it does posterity'll bless our boots for having the guts to stand up and be counted. That's white posterity I'm talking about. You think on it."

Bates sauntered back to the firing line.

Delaverne ground the cigarette out beneath his heel. He did a day's work for a day's dollar; there was no reason why he should feel discontented and threatened in the afternoon, uncertain of the night. He wasn't going to join an organization against police regulations, but if that figure ran across his porch again, he would cut the sonofabitch in half.

He returned to the podium and loaded his revolver. It was a comfortable weapon — totally familiar; only once had he used it on a man, to disable a black assailant in a Dryades Street raid, before he headed up the squad. He carefully shot him in the thigh, and the chief commended him: baptism by fire.

Delaverne took his stand, waited for the instructor's command and then riddled the target with rapid fire, the gun pumping his hand as if in congratulation. Bates smiled grimly; the old warder to Delaverne's right drew back.

"Expecting trouble?" he joked.

"You never know," Delaverne told him.

* * *

"CHRIST, an intellect! I can always finger them. The trouble with you is, Clyde, you dwell too much."

47

The words, rapped out with alcoholic insistence, intruded upon the sedate decrepitude of the Napoleon House. Condemnation: the cosmic judgment. Comiski glanced at his partner's profile as she sipped her Sazerac, recognized the mock gaiety and incipient scorn: she accepted his offer of a drink and the deliberation with which he lit her cigarettes — his bounty — was already resigned to dreary fornication. But first she had to register her disappointment, her preference for something other than a *dweller*. Her presence was a kind of betrayal: he had affection for the bar — a real claim on the muted tile floor, the fans that hung from the ceiling stirring the air and squadrons of lethargic flies, the oil paintings cluttering walls the color and texture of parchment, the sense of graceful aging as if it all were viewed through smoked glass.

"The trouble with you," he said, and didn't finish the sentence. A familiar sound reached him through the doors opened onto the patio — the clatter of tropical leaves in the night wind. It was the sound of summer dying, the gentle expiration of an African sun and the beginning of the rainy season, reminding him of those distant afternoons on the same patio, the feel of a starched shirt glued to his back by perspiration, the cool bitterness of rum and tonic, the warm polished banister spiraling upward toward a friend's apartment where Comiski and his wife once made love, before they were married. There was a view of the river and the rigging of tankers framed against bruised storm clouds sneaking up on the city. He hadn't been prepared, was dutifully afraid of pregnancy, took her with care and precision and retreated at the supreme moment, offering his seed to a breathless humid world. To his surprise he came again and again, until he felt he was turning inside out like

48

a rubber glove; they clung to each other in sleep, in spite of the heat, woke up briefly at the height of the storm, their bodies wet with warm rain blowing in through the window, his dreams disturbed by the broken tempo of sodden plantain leaves lashing the balustrade.

The beginning was so vivid — a cycle of expectation and disaster. The hurricane had saved him: Comiski was forced to work fourteen hours a day for two weeks, and he actually forgot about his wife's leaving. There were so many drowned and bloated bodies that he could smell the morgue from two blocks away; the city was crippled, with hundreds of old shotgun houses shoved off the foundations, the streets of the Ninth Ward covered with ooze left by receding floodwaters. He could still hear the supernatural keening of the killer wind, the pop of windows sucked outward in the fury, the desperate voices of old women who afterward called the newspaper office to complain of rats and alligators in their flower beds, the plea of an exhausted black man in an evacuation center who grabbed Comiski, because there was no one else, to ask what had become of his five children.

The woman leaned against him, said breathily, "You know something? They give me the creeps."

She gestured toward the chess players slumped at the table, absorbed in the positioning of bits of ivory, as if she were dispensing holy water; Comiski spoke in grave stentorian tones.

"Chess, madame, is a venerable contest, one that has been played by rules virtually unchanged for centuries. Awe is the only fitting response to the idea that the contestants march through identical abstract fields of battle as did the ancients."

"It's creepier than I thought," she said.

49

"So stylized has the ritual become that one can't move without committing oneself to an irrevocable course of action, a plan of battle with unknown consequences, in spite of the predictability with which the struggle unfolds."

"Christ, Clyde..."

"My name, madame, is not Clyde."

Comiski acknowledged the patter of applause that rose from the chessboard, placed both hands resolutely on the bar. He had reached the extent of his usual investment; the routine rarely varied — twice a week he sought out women, to ply them with a calculated amount of whiskey and eventually to mount them. They were divorcees from Dallas, errant schoolteachers, and though their coupling was usually a dreary affair, he preferred them to whores.

She was saying, "The trouble with artists and intellectuals and newspaper reporters..."

Comiski herded her outside, tried to imagine her as beautiful, with her brassy hair and sensual legs snared in black knit stockings, her breath moist with bourbon and the essence of orange.

"Where are we going?" she asked.

"To my apartment — one of the lovely restorations of the Vieux Carre. To eat roasted peanuts and watch the antics of Bela Lugosi. To live!"

"That's what you think," she said ambiguously, and climbed into the cab. "Let's go to Dixie's — it's such a gas."

"It's full of queers."

She turned to the window, pouting. They were held up at the corner of Bourbon while two college students thrashed across the headlights, beating each other with their fists. She didn't get out, and he felt her resentment grow as the cab crossed Esplanade and entered the seedier environs of Elysian Fields: junked cars up on concrete blocks, store windows imprisoned behind meshed steel, the clapboard rooming house with sooty geraniums on the porch to which he had been coming home for too many years.

"The prince and his castle," she murmured.

While Comiski searched his pockets for his press card to present to the driver, the woman got out and stood on the curb, cradling her breasts with crossed arms; he joined her, ushered her across the porch and into the house, past the landlady's door and up the stairs in silence.

The entrance was the hardest part. Comiski was reluctant to reveal the disarray of his life: the pile of unfolded laundry, a stack of newspapers beside the couch and the overflowing ashtray on the armrest, the uncapped pint of Jim Beam, the photographs he tore out of magazines and pinned to the wall of the kitchenette with thumbtacks — an actress in a space suit, plastic breast exposed, a popular author chasing a butterfly through a timeless pastoral setting. He never knew exactly why he chose them; the ambivalence seemed indefensible.

The woman noticed nothing. She fingered her curls, smoothed her dress, smiled at Comiski, resigned and drunk, asked, "Where's the ladies'?"

He showed her, was thankful she didn't lock the door. Women do strange things in strange bathrooms. He switched on the closet light, threw the newspapers behind the couch, turned on the television. This must be love, Comiski thought, its inception and glorious fruition. He poured bourbon into an empty jelly glass, remembered there was no ice, took off his raincoat and jacket, and stretched out on the cushions. The newscaster's canned voice told him nothing, droned on and on in what might have been a foreign language.

Comiski drifted. There was a time in Baton Rouge when he bathed with his father, in a room at the end of an open walkway: he would hold Comiski in his arms, wrap a blanket around them both before walking back along the balcony, steam rising from their warm bodies in the early morning air. Comiski remembered swarms of chemical waste between him and the sky, flowers blighted by yellow powder, the reek of burning sulphur from the works. Their house backed up to a bayou as opaque as liquid mud, full of broken crates and old tires and offering sanctuary to millions of swamp mosquitoes and skeletal fish that on warm nights floated on the surface.

But you first saw God, Comiski thought, endured puberty in southern Mississippi. In one of a hundred hamlets with alliterative Indian names, where he was raised by his mother's family and the seemingly endless days of mediocrity were scored with epiphanies of such intensity that he still couldn't escape them. It was the smells that held on forever: magnolia blossoms, red dust baked in the sun, hogs' offal, stewing mustard greens, and salt pork, a young girl's first excitement.

He roused himself, sipped the whiskey. The newscaster had been replaced by animated drawings of space rockets; an astronaut's midwestern rasp let Comiski in on some anecdotes of life in orbit. He turned off the sound, watched the spiny capsules court each other through the reaches of nothingness, hooking up at last like blind fish mating a hundred miles beneath the ocean.

The woman was singing in the bathroom. Comiski got up

and opened the door, saw a strange person with astonishingly white flesh standing naked before his mirror. She had massive thighs and breasts, with nipples the shape and texture of bread sticks; she reached for the ceiling with one hand while shaving her underarm with his straight razor.

"Give me a minute, Clyde," she called out gaily, "and you're going to love me!"

He shut the door in disgust, went back to the couch. I'm not up to it, he thought, I quit. Sex must have once amounted to more than two bodies banging together in the miasmal darkness of his room. He consoled himself with the memory of the first time: Comiski was deflowered by a sharecropper's daughter with dirty toes and total disregard for his sentiments.

The bathroom light blinded him. He could smell the woman's perfume, his own shaving soap, her nakedness; he closed one eye, lay still, staring into the gray infinity of the television screen.

"You're not ready," she said.

She bent over him, one elastic breast brushing his forearm, her flushed and baffled face intercepting his line of vision. He managed not to blink; she muttered, "Christ, Clyde..." and with a sharp intake of breath fled back into the bathroom.

Comiski closed his other eye, listened to the sounds of her frantic dressing: his razor rattled in the basin, her high heels scraped on the tiles, something was overturned as she struggled with an exacting piece of underwear. When she reemerged, he opened an eye, locked in a zombie's stare, realized too late that it was the wrong eye.

The woman didn't notice. She skirted the couch, unwilling to investigate; with a shrug she slipped the pint of bourbon into her purse and went down the stairs, leaving the door open behind her.

Comiski got up and went to the window, pulled the curtains aside. In Algiers a gas flame burned over the refinery, blinked and guttered like a candle in the wind, alone in the middle of the swampy plain; upriver, the bridge seemed to sag beneath the weight of darkness, and the sky was stained a dirty red. Somewhere he had missed out, failed to follow through — it was as simple as that. Comiski had a desire to finish something, to pass through the intestines of some dilemma, however petty, and emerge on the other side, bespattered but finished. Washed up. He was tired of ragged edges.

He watched the woman pause beneath the streetlamp on Elysian Fields and tilt up the bottle; she walked stolidly out of sight. Comiski stared at the grass in the center strip for a while, remarked that the iridescent light stained it purple, and then went back to the couch and fell asleep, without bothering to remove his clothes.

THE SHOW-UP room was crowded with policemen in street clothes. Delaverne sat at the back, avoiding Bates and his friends who stood in a tight group against the far wall, talking through their teeth and watching for the sergeant to take his place. He heard Bates say, "We've had more than enough of this nigger shit. No black boy wants to sit down next to me in Antoine's — it's been proved that niggers don't like a lot of rich food."

Delaverne disliked attending show-ups: the shoddy chairs, walls of black beaverboard, the exhaust fumes from the car pool next door, the glaring lights, and the sergeant's jibes depressed him, reminded him of a strip show that never revealed what the barker promised. The characters that stumbled onto the platform were just what they appeared to be: human garbage — white bums scraped up from Camp Street, black bums jerked out of billiard parlors along Dryades, whores from Decatur, and queers from Bourbon, undesirables from everywhere. If they couldn't be saddled with the crime in question, they would certainly qualify for another. Delaverne wondered why the department bothered to show them at all; in an earlier age they would have simply lined them up and mowed them down. Crows on a fence.

Half a dozen black men shambled onto the platform, squinting into the light. Bates went to join a man and wife and their teen-age daughter who sat in the second row; he smiled, put his arm on the back of the girl's chair, leaned forward and whispered to her father. Both parents looked at the girl, who shook her head, the glossy black hair swirling about her shoulders.

No, Delaverne thought, of course not. How could she recognize him? It was probably dark; she was terrified. He was thankful that he had no children to be tormented by the freaks roaming the face of the earth. His wife had been after him for years to adopt; he had good reason to be reluctant — he *knew*. Delaverne also shrank from the mechanics of adoption, the association of guilt and destitution: if someone could just deposit a child in his wife's arms, without all the rigmarole...

The sergeant called the first suspect forward. The man sidestepped into the light, his shoulders raised in a catatonic shrug; Delaverne noticed that the fly of the man's trousers wasn't buttoned. He wondered if the girl noticed his exposed undershorts. Someone behind Delaverne laughed; he felt the grip of nausea. It was a disgusting display: he was appalled by the access people had to one another, imagined a jumble of human beings of all hues rubbing together, grinning, touching what they were able, breathing up all the oxygen.

Delaverne pushed out into the aisle. He felt sickened, angry, and misused, didn't know why.

The guard at the door whispered, "Your show's on next."

"I need some air," Delaverne said.

Comiski loved the track. Crowded stands beneath a clear autumn sky, the jockeys' silk shirts bright in the sun, the smell of fresh broken earth, beer in paper cups, the post horn heralding each race in strains belonging to a better age, the common heave of thousands of people with the common aspiration to pick a winner — he felt as if he belonged to it all.

Comiski found the fairgrounds, a week before opening day, depressing. The stands were shrouded in faded green canvas; the windows of the press box stared out at an empty board. The track was a scummy morass at the east turn. He picked his way through the weeds toward the complex of stables, where a Negro sat beneath some eaves, his yellow baseball cap tilted forward over his eyes.

"I'm looking for a horse," Comiski told him. "The name's Driven Snow."

The man might not have heard. Comiski noticed the faded red Windbreaker, muddy canvas shoes without laces, felt the anger stir — the old hairy atavism.

"The horse belonged to a man named Parks," he said patiently, adding, "he was a friend of mine."

The man raised his cap and looked up at Comiski; all resemblance to a stableboy disappeared. There was something threatening in the raised scars across his cheeks that might have been ritualistic in their symmetry, the insolent eyes, teeth tipped with gold. He sighted along his arm, said, "Down t'utha end. Numbah foh-teen."

Comiski moved off, aware that the man was watching him; when he reached the stable, he leaned heavily against the sliding door and, before going inside, looked behind him. The Negro was gone.

The touch of the worn wooden latch was familiar: he sorted out the odors of hay, dry manure, horse blankets, and old harness leather, remembered another barn — a dilapidated shell bearing an advertisement for Red Bull chewing tobacco that could be seen from the road. He felt the motionless heat of August in Mississippi, the coolness of chicken droppings oozing between his toes, the hard gnarled boards of the loft against his bare back where he used to lie and stare up at a thousand points of light between spreading shingles. His private stars, eclipsed by the endless coming and going of a pair of swallows that built a clay nest in the rafters. With sudden clarity Comiski knew what life was all about: he must watch out for hornets, cottonmouths, and poison ivy, could go forever on deep-fried catfish steaks and corn bread, had experienced the ultimate satisfaction of a Moon Pie and a Nehi orange at Forshag's drugstore.

A dozen racehorses craned their necks across the barriers, stamped their hoofs as if impatient for Comiski to choose. They were almost indistinguishable in the shadows, and as he walked between them he realized that he wasn't sure what

Parks's horse looked like, or even why he had come. He felt sentimental and foolish, sat down on a stack of empty feedbags, and rested his head against the railing. At least he was safe — out of touch; the semidarkness and the familiar smells, the company of beasts was reassuring. What everybody needed was a barn, a husk to fill with discarded memories and maybe a pig or two, a place to labor and a place to hide.

Comiski put a cigar into his mouth, but didn't light it. He smoked too much, drank too much, indulged himself so that he differed radically from the adolescent he remembered: he used to have muscular forearms from bucking hay bales behind his uncle's tractor, enough energy to work all day and then ride around all night in someone's low-slung oil-devouring Chevy. He smelled the cheap hair lotion, the raw heady smoke of Home Run cigarettes passed from hand to hand, recalled the sense of excitement when five boys piled into the car and careened down darkened gravel roads with mindless speed, bound for nowhere. There was that one dry September night when Comiski sat in the back seat, holding a pumpkin in his lap. He had stolen it from beneath the ramp at the ice house for no particular reason; there was always something that could be done with a pumpkin. The headlights outlined a battered pickup with treadless tires and a shuddering taillight, a hound baying in the truck bed. They overtook it, and Comiski glimpsed the black face in the cab, the stylized grin, white stubble, and sinewy hands gripping the wheel like dead bats. The truck was draped in dust; no one looked behind, yet every person in the car knew what turn the night had taken. They were about to strike a collective blow in the interest of vague social justice: Comiski and his pumpkin had been tapped as the bow and shaft of retribution, without a word being spoken.

The driver swerved off into a side road and reversed before the car had come to a complete halt; with much sliding and spewing of gravel they were off again, in the opposite direction, bearing down on the pickup's feeble headlights. The common excitement was heightened by the knowledge that the Negro had seen their maneuver: they understood the fear inherent in the sight of a car turning around on a secondary road.

Comiski took up his position, thrust his body out of the window, and dragged the pumpkin after him; hands grasped his belt to steady him as he leaned far out into the warm night air full of insects and determination. The truck shook comically, the old motor laboring beyond its capacity; the driver's grin, set after six or seven decades of perseverance, infuriated Comiski, and he leaned far out into the headlights' glare, raised the pumpkin above his head and hurled it forward. The windshield was annihilated with the sound of crushed bone. Comiski's ears were full of the wind and cries of jubilation from the others; he clung to the stanchion of the car window and watched the truck veer off onto the shoulder of the road and nose into the ditch, the lights illuminating a jungle of weeds backed by calm water.

He knew that he was in trouble, couldn't clear his head. The sound of the motorcycles barely reached him, the engines cutting off as one and giving him back his silence; he might not have heard them at all, resolved that all was well. But the shriek of the sliding stable door and the shaft of light were the real determinants. Comiski got clumsily to his feet, confused and afraid, began to mouth apologies to the shadowy figures that approached him. He changed tactics and cursed them. A horse blanket was thrown over him; he was propelled backward and pinned against the railing, while his groin came under attack from a jack-hammer. Comiski recognized, before going down and long before they let up, the professional flurry Grunt must have developed after years of punching the heavy bag.

TEA cut across Broad Street like a man in a trance. He ignored the traffic light and the blue Mustang that sped closely by in a blare of antiphonal horns, instinctively hexed the driver and watched with satisfaction as the white man hit the brakes and turned to snarl at him. Tea moved on: that sort of confrontation no longer interested him, was an indulgence and a kind of unthinking white subversion to keep him from his real purpose — there was no time. Sweat ran from beneath the band of the baseball cap, where his hair was tucked safely out of sight, coursed along the lesions of old scar tissue, soaked the neck of his Windbreaker. His toes protruded through the strips of newspaper lining his tennis shoes, which were caked with mud and horse manure and flopped with each step. He was used to that humiliation, an important facet of his present identity: Tobias Teague, stableboy and chattel — Tea the nigger.

He tried to laugh — a rasp of barely contained impatience and disdain. In the last six months he figured he must have walked thousands of miles. There was never money for cabs, no matter how important the mission; as often as not there was trouble when he rode the bus. White trash to put straight, old women who objected to Tea's hair style, the proximity of the driver's neck, so open and easy and white: his projections of death had upset more than one bus schedule. He didn't want petty trouble, couldn't afford to be picked up now, so he walked. Tea had a tight gait — a lean man in a hurry; he passed most white people unnoticed, but Negroes stepped aside, regarded him with a mixture of amusement and apprehension.

He knew they mocked his haste, could hate them for it, but then they were afraid. Tea was not afraid; the word was that he *moved* — missions of importance. Often it seemed absurd, when he found himself waiting in a stinking project hallway or standing on a corner in the sun: it made him want to laugh, but laughing took time, held him up. He never seemed able to meet the deadlines he set for himself — the meetings, the persuasion, and the hustling, the endless lists of priorities. He always seemed to be, in retrospect, on the street, plagued with anger and frustration that walking enhanced, hurrying, sweating, and late.

He paused in front of a sundry store on the corner of Music. A poster in the window advertised Silky Smooth hair straightener and showed a man photographed in soft focus exposing incredibly white teeth. He had an olive complexion, Caucasian features, and auburn hair that appeared to have been stenciled onto his scalp. Tea stared at the photograph, struggled to obliterate that smile: the time was coming, but before that he had to go through another change, to keep them guessing. It was a logical choice — for a few days longer he would be invisible. The reasoning made him angrier; he gripped the matchbox inside the pocket of his Windbreaker as if it were a bomb, primed and ready, went reluctantly into the store.

A black woman in a flowered kimono stood behind a counter littered with pipe cleaners, shoe polish, and bobby pins, all-day suckers and plastic combs and assorted cheap objects for the momentary brightening of uneventful lives; she glanced once at Tea and looked away.

"You got something to hold it down?" he asked. "Some kind of grease?"

Her hand moved listlessly toward the display of Silky Smooth. Tea shook his head.

"Not that. I want something temporary."

She opened a drawer, took out a tube of pomade covered with silver stars, and pushed it across the counter, drummed on the glass with thick knuckle-less fingers. She could have been his own mother; he wanted to slap her, drag her outside, and show her a few things. She was Tea's own special problem — the Rock. How could he ever move that mass of fatalism and defense mechanisms, how could he free the soul buried beneath layers of religiosity and starch-corrupted flesh? He flicked for the thousandth time through his mental index of filing cards, searching for the missing notation; it didn't surface. Detonation was easy enough — a reliable factor: it had been proven that the woman was capable of an act of aggression. The problem lay in sustaining that aggression. Spontaneity wasn't enough — there were too many distractions. Victory involved accumulation, a ground swell that would feed upon itself, irrevocable once launched; he believed in that victory as he believed in his and in her existence, but the index card was still missing. There was no time.

Tea carefully read the list of ingredients.

"Says here it's scented. Give me something that don't stink."

The woman gazed longingly out into the sunlit street.

"Don't stink, boy. Smells real good."

62

"Shit," said Tea.

Her features became distended, grotesque; her eyes flashed toward the curtained doorway at the back of the store.

"Dat's all we got."

He scattered change over the counter and went out. The autumn sun blinded him, and he cursed himself for never sparing the money, all summer, for dark glasses. He could have written them off as expenses, a new identity — yet another change. The pomade tube felt repulsive in his Windbreaker pocket, stoked his anger. In the distance he could see the concrete facade of the police station: it was some satisfaction — an indulgence — to strike so close to home, to harass the pickets and be gone.

Tea walked steadily until he reached the corner of Benefit. A white woman pushing a shopping cart passed by without seeing him, went into the liquor store; he watched a man come forward to serve her, then stepped into a phone booth, deposited his nickel, and dialed.

The phone rang once; a thick negroid voice said, "Yeah?"

"He been there yet?"

"Yeah, man. He been bein' here."

"You tell him I'm coming."

Tea hung up. He took the matchbox out of his pocket, unwound the heavy rubber band. The box contained three rusty blades from a safety razor; he placed one horizontally between his middle and forefinger and wrapped the rubber band about his knuckles, clamping the blade in place. He was sweating in the closeness of the booth, but his hands were dry. Black man sweats when he works: *nigger don't sweat ain't worth killin'.*

Tea felt a point of heat behind his eyes, spread his lips in a parody of the advertisement for Silky Smooth. Carrie said sweating made him scrawny, that everything came out through his skin. If maybe you could relax. He had no time for relaxation, no time for tobacco, liquor, gigs, and, lately, for sex: she felt the bind of all his abstinence. Even when he touched her he shriveled in a nameless rage, groped for an adversary; Carrie suffered.

Tea watched the woman come out carrying her six-pack of Jax; he waited until she headed up toward Tulane, and then went into the store.

Tiny chimes announced his entrance. A white man in wraparound sunglasses was arranging miniature Scotch bottles on the counter; he came to attention, jammed his fists against his hips.

"Now just a minute here," he said.

"Shut your mouth, fool."

Tea leaned over the counter and took the man's glasses.

"I don't want no misbehaving," he said.

"Why you must be insane. Pick on somebody else — I got my insurance to think about."

"You won't be thinking about nothing unless you get that register open." Tea gripped the pomade tube, pushed it forward against the lining of his jacket. "Move, fool!"

"I ain't gonna do it," the man said. "I ain't just gonna stand here and watch you clean me out again. You just go ahead and shoot me, if that's what you really want."

His voice broke. Tea despised his whining, his limpid blue eyes, the spot of tissue adhering to his neck where he had cut himself while shaving: so open, so easy. He checked himself,

64

reached out, and flicked his fingers; the man gasped, clamped his hand on his forearm, watched with disbelief as blood spread over the white shirt sleeve.

"Aw, hell," he moaned.

"If there's no more than fifty bills," Tea said quietly, "you're dead trash."

The man jabbed at the cash register, dribbled bills among the Scotch bottles; his breath came noisily between slack gray lips.

"Where's the gun?" Tea asked.

"Ain't no gun. I wouldn't give you-all the excuse."

Tea knew it was true: he had miscalculated, counting on this white man to provide him with a weapon — a minor annoyance.

"Now you lie down there on the floor and keep shut."

He stuffed the money into the pocket with the pomade, slashed the coiled telephone wire without touching the receiver. Not a trace of Tobias Teague. He put on the sunglasses, looked down at the owner who lay among the sprinkling of discarded receipts, knees pulled up to his chin; Tea wanted to laugh.

"I'll be back," he said.

He folded the baseball cap and hid it inside his Windbreaker, hurried out. The air felt cool and liberating, but Tea experienced no elation: already the chimes were a memory, the robbery a phenomenon that had occurred too far in the past. He was neither afraid nor excited, just impatient — the others were waiting, and he was late.

A buck-toothed cop on a three-wheel motorcycle crossed the intersection ahead, puttered away in a daydream, instinctively marshaling the afternoon traffic. So close — the only real satisfaction. Tea climbed into an ancient Plymouth waiting at the Negro cabstand, told the driver to take him across town; he figured he had twelve minutes to get clear.

The old man scratched the expanse of freckled pate, studying him in the mirror, folded his paper, took an eternity to set the meter and get the car in motion. Tea was exhausted. He fingered the bills in his pocket, decided not to count them; he took out the matchbox, replaced the blade and rubber band, and stowed the kit in his sock. He located his list for the day — a scrap of damp note paper — unfolded it and began to check off the items with a pencil stub:

1. Cover stable/see who feeds horse

2. Hit juice shop

3. PM connect/Clarence's. Fix arms deliver no later/ Wed.

4. Explain Jupe/concept black proletariat and (last time) concept detonate and cumulative affect

5. Buy food

6. Find Carrie

He turned the paper over to begin a list for the following day; he considered, then wrote:

1. Cover white man's crib. Some connect/Parks

Tea replaced the paper and pencil, told the driver to stop. As he paid, he heard a siren start to wail far up Tulane Avenue; he got out and walked quickly toward the river. His stride was habitual, mesmerizing. Time was still the enemy — life was waste; he wondered if he would ever make it, would ever take part in the real thing. Tea saw his own life as a series of confrontations without any real consequence, a lost cause. The greatest waste was the year spent in the reading room of the University of Chicago library, studying the white man; he had a forged pass and occasionally hustled grass laced with oregano among the students to supplement the money Carrie made in the automat. But most of the time he read, demolishing book after book in his own erratic fashion; he understood little of what he read in the beginning, forgot most of that, but with a determination that brought him close to insanity he forced himself to pass his eyes over the words in those volumes he set before himself. He disposed of much of Rousseau, Pascal, and Marx, Freud, Rimbaud, and even Faulkner: somewhere, he was certain, there was an explanation — a delineation of the system by which supremacy is attained.

The explanation never materialized, unless it was the very process of obscuring truth with proliferation and detail. The opacity of the texts fueled his rage and his determination; when the year was up, Tea had only regrets. He was no longer sure which ideas were his own and which belonged to the verbose white men he had studied. He glimpsed the method, if not the origins, of power: they had gained subtle control of his mind, while teaching him nothing of value — he was tainted. The absurdity of his position was apparent in the simple fact that Tea had never taken part in a protracted civil disorder. Since he was a boy growing up around Shakespear Park, violence had been the common denominator in his life, but that violence was mostly directed against his own kind and linked with the attainment of property and status. Violence led to a modicum of success: black man preyed upon black man in emulation of the white man's concept of supremacy and individual worth. Tea marveled at the ingenuity of suppression. He aimed to change all that — he was bringing the real thing home.

He entered the upheaval of the Loyola slum clearance

project, moved between mutilated tenements and piles of rubble. He knew Carrie was there, somewhere, listening to the radio, drifting: he didn't have much time with her, either. Tea remembered the days behind the Loop and a wide-eyed country girl fresh from Plaquemines, lying on the floor of a stolen Imperial convertible, too terrified even to look at the fresh slash marks across his cheeks that turned inside out like gutted blood sausage. He could laugh then, yet he was hurt that she didn't appreciate his sacrifice, couldn't understand the extent of his commitment. Scars are forever; curiously, they dated him. A new concept of integrity had evolved since then — the black body beautiful — and his badges of defiance made him old before his time, still waiting for the fire, uninitiated in any meaningful sense.

With whispered obscenities he picked his way across the razed lot, entered the clapboard cafe.

Colored bulbs were strung across the rafters, gathering dust and cobwebs since a forgotten Christmas; a black man at the back table stood and adjusted his tie, smiled vacantly. Tea knew he was dreaming of the days when petty black politicians held banquets in the rooms upstairs, like their white counterparts in the Roosevelt Hotel, and he despised him for it.

"Hey, man," said Clarence.

Tea nodded, went up the steps two at a time and hurried along the corridor. Blues music came from a hidden transistor radio, and for a moment he thought he heard a baby's cry; he opened the door marked TESTIMONIALS.

Jupe sat hunched forward in a chair next to the window, his head bobbing as he tottered on the threshold of consciousness, long legs thrust beneath the table; he caught sight of Tea, stood in a spasm of angular limbs, went through his shuffle.

"Hold still!" Tea told him.

Jupe grinned. "Dis here's Calvin."

"Hey, man." Calvin stood up, raised a clenched fist.

Tea registered distaste, refused to raise his own. He disliked the African talisman dangling from Calvin's neck, the charcoal mohair suit, the unstraightened but closely cropped hair, the ready smile, and the air of manicured anonymity.

"So you finally made it 'round."

"Sho," Calvin said. "I been hearing all 'bout you, Prince."

"That right? Now what you got to offer?"

Calvin turned up well-scrubbed palms, began to enunciate. "We're featuring several items at this particular moment. I'm here to help out — you just tell me what it is you need."

"You can help me out with four dozen grenades."

Calvin shook his head. "No grenades, Prince. But we got something a whole lot better. We're featuring at this particular moment bazookas."

"Bazookas? Shit!"

"Shee-hut!" Jupe echoed.

"Cuts ole Whitey in half ever time," Calvin said. "Guaranteed to please."

"You talk like some kind of a fool. Can you see me breezing down Desire toting a bazooka? You're some help, man."

Calvin's smile faded. "Well, we got these here little fire bombs, if that's where you're at at this particular moment. Nitro-sumpum'anuthah in Alka-Seltzer bottles. Put one on Whitey and he turns to cracklin.'"

"You got a line of jive for everything."

"We like to present our items in the best light, Prince.

That's our policy."

"That right? Well I'll take fifty Alka-Seltzer bottles and four machine guns."

"Let me reiterate," Calvin said, "that I'm here to help out. But I don't deal for no U.S. Army, and machine guns my firm don't got. We do have some mighty fine little carbines, mighty handy. Whitey don't know you got one stuck down your pants leg, not till you pull it out and ventilate him."

"Four carbines, then, and a thousand rounds. That should get us off the ground."

"Mighty fine," Calvin said.

He smiled pleasantly, but didn't move; Tea took the crumpled bills out of his pocket and tossed them onto the table.

"Down payment," he said. "I want the stuff by Tuesday or Wednesday — no later."

"I can't do much dealing with this change. Prices go up with credit."

"You talk like the company store."

"We got high overhead, Prince."

"That right? Well just let me pull your coat, Mistah Entrepreneur — there's more bread coming into this brotherhood than you ever thought about. Now if I was you, I'd take a chance."

Calvin gathered up the money. "I'll see what they say."

"You do that thing."

"Yeah," said Jupe.

Calvin buttoned his jacket, moved to the door.

"No call to fight," he said. "We're all in this together."

"That right?"

70

Tea waited until he was gone, turned on Jupe.

"What'd you tell that man?"

"Nuthin' much. Tol' him bettah not mess witch you." Jupe furrowed his brow: his expression of seriousness. "Hey Prince, we gwine talk?"

"Not now. I got to think." Tea handed across the last bill. "Find Sis and give her that, tell her to eat. I'll be along later."

Jupe got up reluctantly, paused at the door. "Hey Prince," he said. "Wha's a *entre-manure?*"

"A kind of white man. Get on now."

Tea sat alone at the banquet table, waited for the sound of his lieutenant's footsteps to die away; he took a small blue loose-leaf notebook from his back pocket and thumbed through it. The final entry read, "273 — Injection of a large sum of capital into movement/ dangerous implications. Isolates administrator from his brothers, has over has not. Aligns adminis. with white status quo/ corrupts. Black trust fund for dispensation top priority."

Tea chewed on the pencil stub, then began to write:

274 — Elimination of middle man. Agent degrades all parties/ corrupts. Consumer to deal direct with supplier.

275 — Hungry people learn fast.

276 — To be hated/ to be free.

He hesitated: that wasn't always true. He drew a line through the last entry, put away the notebook, ran his fingers over his scarred cheeks. To be hated was also to hate. Who then was free? Tea couldn't make the argument jibe, found himself confused: *if that's where you're at at this particular moment...* Had he overlooked some alternative?

He faltered, groped for support. The point of light kindled

in his brain — the footlights of his own private aurora; he welcomed the routine of memory as undeniable reality, the vision of rectitude and purpose. After years of recollection the scene was so familiar that Tea had obtained a position of omniscience, gazing down upon the childish figure of himself and the others with what felt like objectivity. He saw four people: a black boy lay in a pool of urine in the back of a paddy wagon, while two policemen bent over the kneeling figure of a black man on the tailgate. The cops' voices were filled with entreaty as they raised their clubs with the wooden gestures of fat men hampered by tight-fitting clothes, brought the clubs down alternately. The night air was full of the musty odor of chrysanthemums and a sound like that of watermelons being split with an ax. The wagon ground along in low gear; the streetlight showed the sweat stains on the cops' shirts, their faces flushed with exertion. Then one of them beat a funereal tattoo on the metal siding with the flat of his hand. The paddy wagon slowed to a crawl; the cops sidled backward, heaving at their holsters, while the black man pulled himself up by the wagon's iron handles and clung to them. It was Tea's father, and Tea knew they were going to kill him, couldn't believe that he would meekly await the settling of his fate; for that he never forgave him — resist or share the guilt. *Jump, boy. Jump!* The cops advanced again with a dancing motion, legs widespread for balance, chopped with the butts of their pistols; Tea saw his father's knuckles laid bare, watched him drop into the street as if he were suffering nothing worse than humiliation. The cops' haunches collided as they got into position; they fired from the hip, rocking with the reports. Tea's father threw up one arm and then the other but didn't go down, ran on after them, carried forward after death by the wagon's momentum and, once, seemed to be grasping for the tailgate. When he did fall it was with total finality — heap of flesh and bones, his head bouncing on the curb.

He come on like a mad dog. More like the devil...

Tea heard a movement in the hallway. He got up and flung open the door; Clarence's teen-age daughter stood in the shadows, smiling, touching her soft dark hair. He saw that she wore lipstick, white women's clothes.

"Wha's y'all doin' in dare?" she asked.

Tea grabbed her arm and shook her, took the matchbox out of his pocket and pressed it against her cheek.

"Wake up, girl!" he hissed.

She pulled away, fled down the stairs. Tea heard the mellifluous voice of Ray Charles drift up from the juke box, and the sound of black men's laughter — at the same time gay and mournful, totally uncommitted. At least he had his memory.

Tea took out the tube of pomade, opened it, and squeezed the pungent grease into the palm of his hand; cursing softly and persistently, he applied it to his hair.

COMISKI did not want to die. It had nothing to do with pain: he was bothered by the helplessness of a corpse. The idea of Gomer cutting him open with that length of surgical steel was intolerable, as was the vision of his hands on Comiski's heart; he could imagine Gomer probing his innards to determine the makeup of his last meal, to see how many drinks he had and when he last indulged in sex. The autopsist and his microcephalic assistant would play cat's cradle with Comiski's intestines. He could hear the cynicisms as they examined his various members, measured his girth, shoved him naked and violated into a refrigerator like a gutted goose into a cold oven.

He hadn't moved for almost two days. Twice he watched the lights that clung to the underside of the bridge like a dwindling specie of luminous blue mollusk drop off with morning; he was grieved by their extermination, although it meant he had survived another night. Twice he witnessed the arc lights along Elysian Fields resisting the dawn, burning on in defiance of the earth's turning, dying a fanatic's sudden death as the sun's rays touched the pupil of a mechanical eye and tripped the switch.

Comiski's lower abdomen and groin were one livid bruise; he refused to look at it, felt like a condemned man with the execution already under way. *A current of electricity of sufficient strength and magnitude shall pass through your body until you are dead, dead, dead...*

Why three times dead? The first time Comiski heard the death sentence pronounced he was appalled by the theatrics in which the judge indulged: divested of his robes, he was just another hard-drinking politician with too many veins in his nose, who every Christmas Eve ordered the best banjo picker in the Parish Prison brought to his chambers, to play while the judge and his cronies roared out dirty songs. That trial seemed like a poorly acted television soap opera; the defendant, an inarticulate Negro named Justine, accepted the sentence as if it were an accolade. Comiski never doubted his guilt, was convinced that he had murdered a white man with intent, beating him on the head for half an hour with a board while black people hung out of the project windows, alternately encouraging and admonishing him. He could imagine Justine taking time off for a soft drink and a smoke, wiping his brow as he returned to the task, laboring over the body with the same unthinking determination with which he had always stoked furnaces or picked cotton or driven stakes into the ground. The retribution seemed curiously of a kind.

Comiski had paid his own fare on the Trailways up to Angola to witness the execution. He had watched the dreary Louisiana countryside slide past, afraid and yet admittedly exhilarated by the prospect of seeing a man killed. The prison was a ramshackle penal colony that smelled of carbolic soap; Comiski and a handful of other men — prison officials and politicians from upstate — were herded into a bare hall with barred windows, their feet clattering against the floor of the gallery like the rout of a drunken army. Two guards carried Justine in like an unstrung puppet, his head shaved and gleaming, strapped him into the hideous contraption. In spite of the judge's command, the electric current did not prove to be of sufficient strength and magnitude: Justine jerked loose one arm, screamed with perfect enunciation, "Look'a here — dat hurts!"

Comiski watched in horror as the guards grappled with him, strapped down the arm, covered his wrists and ankles and the top of his head with grease to improve the conduction, stepped up the current, and killed him with an overdose. Justine was reduced to a flailing vegetable and broke a leg strap before subsiding. Comiski could never forget the sense of loss, or the odor of scorched rubber, as if a frayed lamp cord had blown a fuse and filled the room with darkness.

Tea pushed open the door. Morning sunlight filtered through shreds of tufted gauze curtain, revealed a dark stain in one corner of the room. An iron bedstead stood in the middle of the floor, flanked by a doorless armoire piled with yellowed copies of the *Times-Picayune;* a rat trap lay discarded in the sink. Cockroaches, panicked by the intrusion, spread over the wall like shrapnel diffusing in slow motion outward from the point of detonation, disappearing beneath the molding, behind hanging strips of wallpaper, down the drain. There was a smell of abandonment: cold ashes in the stove, grease gone solid in the pan, leaking water pipes, the remains of a dozen boiled and picked buster crabs.

"Just like home," he said, dumping the cardboard suitcase and the battered clock radio onto the bed. "Just like old times."

"Some home," Carrie said. "This has got to be the bottom."

She unburdened herself of the Schwegmann's shopping bag, and it toppled, spilling socks, a carton of cigarettes, and a yellow baseball cap onto the soiled ticking of the mattress. She sat among their belongings, licked the tip of one thumb, and began to massage the light discolored flesh in the crook of her elbow: it was numb.

"They got us coming and going, Tea. They sure got us on the run."

"Nobody's running — we're just laying up, that's all. We're just getting off the street for a day or two."

Carrie didn't look up, knew he would feel obliged to convince her.

"I know a man bringing guns — then we'll see who's on the run." He added, "You don't care, anyway."

She felt empty, thick-headed, and close to sleep: that

particular lie was too much of an effort.

"No," she said. "I don't much care."

"You trying to kill yourself, girl?"

She laughed, shook her head, found that she hadn't made a sound; the bush of unstraightened hair danced before her eyes.

"I got burned, that's all. A man at Clarence's put me on to some bad shit — a mistake."

Tea said, "You ought to watch yourself."

She touched his arm: the skin felt hot and unforgiving, looked ebony compared with the jaundiced hue of her own.

She asked, "Where you been?"

"Dealing."

He stepped to the window, jerked the curtain aside, and held up a handful of shredded cloth. The boom of a wrecking crane was visible at the end of the block, stilled by the Sabbath; the convoluted steel and concrete of the expressway glinted in the sun.

"What's become of your baby?" he asked.

"My baby," she said, "belongs to welfare."

She had practiced that answer until it seemed too easy; Tea didn't even notice.

"You got the stash?"

"I got it," she said.

"Big plans, Sis — real plans, for once. When the man comes, things'll pop. We got our work cut out."

Carrie lit a cigarette with a hand that wouldn't be hurried, dropped the match onto the linoleum.

"I'm tired already," she said.

COMISKI opened the bathroom window and pushed his face out into the night air thick with the smell of roasting coffee beans and the oily scud blowing in from the river. He had missed work that morning, spent much of the afternoon cleaning shredded vegetables from the ceiling, after he placed a can of chop suey in boiling water and it exploded. He was drawn toward the lights, the taste of real food, and a drink mixed by other hands.

A Negro loitered in front of the hardware store across the street, his back against the steel mesh shielding the window. Only a black man could stand like that, Comiski reflected — motionless, contained, devoid of aspirations and illusions, going nowhere and not obliged to appear as if he were. Comiski recognized him as the stableboy who, sometime after the beating, had helped him half-conscious into a cab. Since then he had disposed of the yellow baseball cap and added a pair of sunglasses to his ensemble, a conceit that would have been laughable if it hadn't lent him the aspect of a Tonton Macoute, associated with political murders and activities in darkened graveyards. His hair was set flat against his head, and it glistened in the light of the streetlamp. As Comiski watched, the man turned and walked away toward the docks; he didn't look back. Peace go with you, Comiski thought, our parley — now at an end — was strictly circumstantial. He shaved gingerly, avoiding the welt beneath his temple; he dressed like an arthritic old man — fumbling with the buttons on his shirt, straining to reach his shoelaces. The bourbon bottle he avoided. Before going out he remembered the black man, and he went back into the bathroom, wiped the blade of his straight razor clean, and slipped it into his raincoat pocket.

The street was deserted; he crossed the corridor of Elysian Fields with shoulders hunched, hands in his pockets, felt like a man prepared for bad weather.

Bourbon Street was warming. The barkers emerged from the strip clubs like drowsy lice drawn by the darkness, regarded Comiski with lifeless eyes, didn't waste their pitch; a fresh-faced sailor at the end of a day's pass sat on the curb in front of Todd's Steak House, vomiting between outstretched legs. Comiski went inside, secluded himself behind a ragged cane partition, and ordered a drink and a Texasburger. While he ate he watched a bar girl with a platinum ponytail and a fine hard mouth lay waste to a pound of sirloin. She never once spoke to the glabrous Mason from Dallas who harangued her with descriptions of his air-conditioned cruiser and was left to pay.

It began to rain. As Comiski went out he pulled up the collar of his coat; umbrellas bloomed like perverse black flowers in the drizzle, and he moved among their spiny extremities. He wanted to scream, to crush something small and brittle beneath his heel, instinctively ran a thumb along the smooth cold casing of the razor. In front of him, slumped against a wall in the shelter of a marquee, was the figure in the sunglasses and faded Windbreaker; at the sight of Comiski he moved off toward Canal, hunching his shoulders against the rain.

Comiski followed him. The Negro seemed content with the reversal of roles, tarried in front of the clubs to scrutinize the blown-up photos of silicone breasts and pubic areas stamped with a triangle of sequins. He turned on Bienville, and Comiski stayed with him until they reached Rampart, moved up and stood beside him, in front of a pawn shop and a display of switchblade stilettos stuck into a wooden leg;

79

together they studied a cracked ivory handle carved with the figure of a mermaid, a silver button for her navel, a rusty serpentine blade for a tail. Comiski felt oddly at ease, full of curiosity. He wondered what sort of weapon his mark carried, imagined him pulling one of the homemade implements the police confiscated — a belt studded with slivers of steel, a contraption fashioned from pipe and strips of inner tube to propel the spike of an icepick through some unsuspecting brain.

The black man smiled. He turned and hurried across Rampart, hailing a bus; Comiski followed, the muscles in his groin protesting, stepped up and stood behind him while he fumbled for change. The odors of the stables, sweat, rain, and brilliantine were interchangeable. Comiski felt pity for the skinny sodden figure picking out his pennies, sitting defiantly in the foremost seat of the bus.

They got down together in the wasteland of the Loyola Street slum clearance. Comiski surveyed the heaps of rubble, the half-wrecked tenements with exposed staircases leading to infinity, toilets hanging in midair. The doorways of buildings that hadn't yet fallen were filled with inscrutable black faces; transvestites in glossy wigs and satin gowns that trapped the light in fluctuating electric z's clustered in an alleyway and whistled to him, laughed and cursed him softly.

The man smiled at him again, entered a tenement. Madness, Comiski thought; he remembered a police cadet training course on psychology he once attended, and a white instructor who insisted upon using the possessive pronoun. *What your white man most fears is entrapment inside the black community. Your white man will under no circumstances enter a*

80

darkened place where your black man might be hovering...

"Starkers," Comiski said aloud. "Starkers and ravers."

He smelled the rats before he heard them: a musty clinging odor, furious scrabbling behind the baseboard. At the head of deserted stairs burned a pale green light. He ran a single finger up the banister, gripped the clasped razor inside his pocket; the insides of his biceps were slick with perspiration.

The man waited on the landing: the sunglasses and the smile were gone. He watched Comiski's ascent, one hand hanging limply in the pocket of his Windbreaker. Comiski stepped past him, turned so that the Negro's back was to the stairs; he remembered the scars, the insolent eyes. "What's going on?" he asked.

The man made a sound like laughter. "You come up behind me when I'm backing into my crib and ask me what's happening. You come over here through the rain and all that drag out yonder — the only spook that's ever been up these pissy stairs — just to ask me what's happening. That's some shit."

It wasn't the voice Comiski heard at the stables: the menial — the slurred southern idiom of subservience and dogged respect — had been transformed. A hateful precision honed each phrase to the edge of insult: it was a voice picked up in a northern ghetto that would drive certain policemen to excess.

"From this side," the man went on, "it looks like you asked once too often what's happening. Looks like somebody leaned on you."

"All right," Comiski said, "you're a real fact-finder. Maybe you can tell me why those punks beat me up."

"We got no truck together. I wouldn't care if that bunch of white trash rubbed your gray ass right out."

81

"Tea!"

Comiski saw a girl standing in the open doorway, holding a terrycloth robe about her with thin bare arms; she stepped back out of sight, but her shadow lay across the corridor, climbed the opposite wall.

"Now watch your manners, fool," the black man said.

Comiski preceded him into the room. The girl stood against the iron bedstead, clutching the robe as if the idea of him glimpsing her flesh was repulsive; she had light, almost translucent skin — what Delaverne would call a "yaller" — and dense unstraightened hair.

"Tea says you were a friend of Parks's." She rapped the words out; her hands trembled.

"An acquaintance," Comiski said.

"Tea says they stomped you."

"He should know — he watched."

Tea muttered, "Fool," and went over to the sink, where he began to wash his hair beneath the faucet, without removing the Windbreaker.

Comiski said, "I was just asking what's happening. It seemed like a logical question."

"Nothing much happening, Mistah Comiski." She pronounced his name with malice: maybe Parks had always done the same. "Nothing but white folks beating up on white folks. But maybe that's something, after all."

She reached across to the dressing table for a cigarette, and he saw the patch of track marks on the inside of her arm; one of the punctures was raised and inflamed. Meth, he decided, and he envied her, wished he could share the stimulus: the room depressed him, with its scarred furniture and the radio mended

82

with adhesive tape. He had the impression these people were on the move, might beat him to the door. His body ached; Comiski closed his eyes.

"Watch it," Tea said. "The fool's nodding."

He grasped Comiski about the waist, eased him toward the bed.

"You feel like passing, man, you go outside."

Comiski sat, pressed his palms against the mattress. His head throbbed, and his mouth was dry; he knew better than to ask for a drink.

"A result of war injuries," he said.

No one laughed. Tea murmured, "I been to that war," and began to dry his hair with a faded towel; the girl propped herself against the bedstead, smoking with constricted movements, staring down at him with eyes that appeared to be all pupil.

"Tell me who broke into Parks's grave."

The black people looked at each other, and the girl smiled. It was an indication of victory: Comiski had revealed something.

"So that's what brought you round. Now that's some shit."

"Some shit," Tea echoed.

"Those aren't answers," Comiski said. "It may be a stupid question, but nobody likes having his head pushed in for asking stupid questions."

"It must'a been Knee-grows," Tea mocked. "We all know a *Knee*-grow would just as soon bust up another *Knee*-grow's grave as knock over some spook juice shop."

"You worried about freedom of the press and all that?" the girl asked. "Ain't that noble? Well, if you really want to write a story, Mistah White Newspaper Reportah, you can write one about how that bunch of honkie runts is grabbing on to a horse that rightfully belongs to a poh lil' ole black girl." She threw the cigarette into the corner. "If you want to do something, paddy boy, put the heat on them for a change."

"You mean Parks's horse belongs to you?"

"The man just can't believe it, Tea. Let me tell you, man, that I used to *live*. You think this is my scene? Shit! Why, when Parks was around we had a pad out on the lake. Gentilly, no less."

She bent over Comiski, bubbles of saliva collecting at the corners of her mouth; she spread her arms, and the robe fell away, revealing the thrust of a breast and the dark distended nipple. Somewhere, he thought, she must have a child.

The girl shrieked, "I'm going to pull your coat about something so big, so wonderful..."

"Okay, Sis, that's it."

Tea grabbed her arm and sat her in the chair; he jabbed with one finger at the robe until she gathered and held it.

"Your time's up," he told Comiski.

Tea hustled him out into the hall, paused to tie a black scarf around his head; he pulled on tight leather gloves. Comiski shoved his hands into his raincoat pockets, clenched them: the razor was gone.

"Move," Tea said.

He followed Comiski down the stairs and out onto the street, directed him across to the bus stop.

"Don't you worry," he taunted. "We won't let none of these *Knee*-grows mess with you. You never know what a *Knee*-grow might do, once you give him some inches."

Comiski waited on the curb. He was afraid: his visit had changed something. Tea stood behind him, leaning against a brick wall, beneath the inscription, LUKE IS DEAD, STUFF GOT HIM. Black people came out of the shadows to stare at them.

"Now you watch yourself," Tea told him, when the bus came into sight.

"I want my razor back," Comiski said.

"Why, razors are passé, man — don't use them." He touched Comiski's arm: the gesture people reserve for invalids, to show they aren't afraid of contracting disease. "Now that you know the score, you forget about us."

Comiski admitted, "I don't know a thing."

"You're better off," Tea said.

LITTLEBIT pressed his face against the screen, peered out into the alley. He could see nothing, drew back from the stench of brackish salt water and chicken droppings; the lamp on Magazine blazed like a false sun, its emanation denied by the roof's overhang, as if the light itself were wary of penetrating that netherworld. He heard something move: crumbling masonry, oyster shells settling in a barrel — an incongruous sound, amplified by silence. It was late. The landlady's television set in the room above had lapsed into static half an hour before; cars passed infrequently.

Littlebit called throatily, "Git your ass away from that bike!"

His voice sounded distant and unreal; he listened, then went back to the lavatory. The sound could have been anything — kids from Tchopitoulous trying to steal his mirrors, Bud or Grunt or Hoppy checking to see that he hadn't run, one of the obese rats that hung around the garbage cans. The capsule was waiting on the edge of the basin. He placed it on his tongue, drank off a glass of warm water: that would get it working, prime him for the long trip ahead. Littlebit wasn't sure exactly where he was going, planned to ride across the causeway and start navigating when the lake was behind him.

He sat on the edge of the mattress, folded his hands. His belongings were stuffed into a ditty bag hidden under the bed; seventy-three dollars and a gross of amphetamine were secluded inside his army surplus canteen, and his toilet articles were neatly arranged on the shelf below the mirror. He congratulated himself on that bit of ingenuity: anyone checking his room would think that he had just stepped out for a Pepsi and a Lucky Dog, wouldn't suspect that Littlebit was gone forever. He wondered if he was going to miss the city — there had been some good times. Littlebit felt his throat contract, the threat of tears; in a quaking child's soprano he began to sing:

Crawfish pie, jambalaya, filé gumbo,
Son of a gun, we'll have big fun
On the bayou...

He thought he heard someone breathing, got up and switched on the overhead light, peered again through the screen. He saw only a tub of carps' heads and severed chicken feet — monstrous creatures amazed in the midst of an orgy — decided that it was time to be gone. The others were up at Mary's, talking percentages at a back table without bothering to consult him: Littlebit knew his usefulness — his talent — would cease to be of any value once the connection was made. Win, place, or show, it didn't matter — the appearance was the thing. Some torpedo would be flying down from Louisville with the money; it was an elaborate setup, a lot of bread. Bud and the others were dreamers, making big decisions, threatening people when they hadn't even found the stuff: cutting the pie before it's baked. And what if the spades brought it off alone? Now that would be something.

He turned off the light, pulled his gear from beneath the bed, and crept out into the hallway. The landlady would still be awake, listening and scheming. The bitch. She wouldn't let him be, even after she tried to get cute and he shoved her down the stairs; she might even be spying for the others. Littlebit made an obscene gesture in the darkness, slipped out into the street. Magazine looked deserted. The labor of heartfelt rock-a-billy carried all the way down from Mary's; he would have to be quick.

Littlebit paused at the mouth of the alley, hugged the ditty bag. He wanted a place to rest and breathe easy — for it all to be finished. Stasis, a touch of warmth, the annihilation of antagonists: equipoise. His stomach murmured, strained the drug into his blood; he squared his shoulders, and walked into the shadow.

Oh, the smell of her...

Comiski couldn't remember to whom the line belonged; the words recurred like a popular song, haunting his reverie, interrupting his drinking. The Habana was crowded with Latin American seamen who, like himself, were trying to forget that it was only Monday night; the blare of cornets swooped and skittered as a brown man with a gold ring in one ear tilted the juke box from side to side. No one seemed to mind, certainly not Comiski. He had once been a seaman himself, signing on for six weeks with a Belgian freighter delivering guano to Caracas; in those days he could romanticize about riding a pile of bird dung into the sunset. The ship was buzzed by a Mexican fighter plane because Comiski forgot to raise the flag; he contracted gonorrhea in Puerto Barrios and was given a penicillin shot by a nun, lost fifteen pounds sleeping in a secluded oven beneath the engines.

He saw a puffy discolored face in the blue-tinted mirror behind the bar, told it, "I have plowed the main couched in gull shit."

His neighbor held a toothless mongrel on his lap; they stared at Comiski with undisguised hatred.

"Fowl droppings," Comiski said. "Little bitty balls of dookie." He rubbed his hands together.

"I never," the man said.

The barmaid paraded past with a crudely carved wooden phallus, acknowledging the whistles and catcalls, placed it on the bar in front of Comiski. He wondered what he had done to deserve such ingratitude.

"That's revolting," he said.

The barmaid chirped, *"Chinga su madre!"*

"Fuck you in the heart," he rejoined, and that seemed to satisfy her: she took the monstrous dildo away.

"I never in my life," his neighbor said.

Comiski recalled the smells of honeysuckle, spring onions, skunk cabbage, and puffballs crushed beneath his heel that released an acrid swarm of spores, remembered sitting astride his bicycle at the age of twelve, in the middle of the Mississippi night, overcome by the sense of things growing. The crickets' din was disturbed by lilting black girls' voices; he saw the outlines of their cheap crinoline dresses as they came down the path behind the icehouse, avoiding the brambles, bound for the Mount Eternal Church of God, Jesus, Joseph, and Mary. They discovered him, ringed him around, touched him. Comiski struck out, turned from side to side in confusion, angered by their mockery and terrified by the exposure — as if by prearrangement — of dark precocious breasts. From the church came the sonorous chords of an ancient untuned piano and the hymning of black people too powerful for the clapboard structure to contain.

Comiski climbed down from his stool, pushed out through the crowd.

A pickup truck clattered down Decatur, bound for the French Market with a load of Creole tomatoes; the farmer drove in second gear, gawking at all the iniquity. Comiski waved to him, crossed the street on a carpet of broken glass to avoid the Lucky Dog vendor stationed outside the Acropolis — the worst of omens. Two drunks were amiably trying to roll each other beneath the loading ramp of the Jax brewery, while a third crept into the back seat of a tourist's Buick to pass out. Somewhere a juke box shuddered beneath the relentless beat of "Bend It"; two blocks over a siren whooped and wailed.

He could count on four hours of sleep. Then he would do a black girl a small favor, declare himself forever rid of Parks and his remains.

The pale green moon hung above the flood wall. No sound came from the river: the wings were empty.

Oh, Comiski thought. The smell of her.

PART 2:

Jump boy, jump...

DELAVERNE surveyed the corpse. At first he thought it was a child: grubby little toes, clenched fists, white hairless legs. The neck wound resembled an extra mouth, leering and grotesquely comical, exposing the larynx; the blood had been sponged away. Gomer said reverently, "Only a nigger cuts like that." The detective from Homicide motioned for the drawer to be shoved back into the refrigerator; he and Delaverne strolled to the door of the morgue.

"The captain thought you'd be interested," the detective said. "That one won't be bothering your boys anymore."

"Suppose not," Delaverne said. "He was small fry. It's getting where a white boy can't hustle a little cannabis without a black boy knowing about it."

"That's a fact."

"I don't mind if the white pushers and the black pushers want to knock one another off — that's a good balance of nature. But things are getting one-sided."

"It's a problem," the detective agreed.

91

"Let me know what you come up with."

"Will do. That blade was pretty clean."

Delaverne pushed out into the corridor. He had a problem, all right — the dead man might be small fry, but the others weren't, not if his hunch was right. Carefully he examined the components, tried to construct an equation, resisted the anger that was mounting so early in the morning. Negroes start off as consumers, make the natural step up to pushing, get uppity, and break into imports; the stuff floated up the river free as a breeze from Central America, and the federals did next to nothing about it. All that money. He remembered the raid on the white frame house on Washington Avenue, when they busted three blacks and confiscated thousands of dollars in cash concealed in suitcases and half a million dollars' worth of raw heroin in a plastic shopping bag. Delaverne had thrust his fingers into a powdery substance like talcum; it was odorless, tasteless except for a faint trace of quinine. The chief posed in his office for the news media, the cash spilling over his desk — a heroic gesture. At another time the raid might have been played down, and he and the chief would be wealthy men. Things had changed: this time the Justice Department collected.

Delaverne staged his own ceremony for the media — following the chief's example. His men assembled in the basement of the police station, threw boxes of pills and bushels of unmanicured marijuana into the incinerator; Delaverne himself tossed in the bag of heroin. A cloud of thick yellow smoke drifted low over the neighborhood, and before the photographers and reporters could disperse, six automobile accidents were reported in as many square blocks. That was a time of great embarrassment; his career might have been affected, if the chief hadn't backed him.

So much money. For every bundle Delaverne and his men intercepted, fifty, a hundred — a thousand — passed on; he had a vision of banded cash choking an obsolete sewer, just waiting to be spent. What if they got organized and used it to buy off federal judges, politicians, those FBI agents who all sounded like defense lawyers? What if they used that money to hire an army? He tried to decide who would form the ranks of that army: Communists, a certain type of foreigner, blacks, students, and freaks. There seemed to be people everywhere eager and willing to resist the police, to actually attack officers of the law with weapons and with filth. Delaverne could take a certain amount of abuse, prided himself upon his control — it was part of the job. But if a man ever assaulted him with a bag full of crap, he would cut the sonofabitch in half.

He paused outside the Narcotics Bureau. The mechanical rhythm of the mimeograph machine reached out to him — the sound of efficiency. This was his inner sanctum: cramped quarters jammed with filing cabinets, steel-topped desks, old lab equipment that housed the elite. Under Delaveme's methodical leadership, the men snatched the laurels of distinguished service from the hands of the boys in Vice. There were six top detectives and Delaverne's secretary — an adoring old woman saved from the drudgery of the traffic violations files. His men were young and unafraid; two of them had killed.

Delaverne went in. A pair of detectives sat at the table in their shirt sleeves — their shoulder straps and holsters like braces for improving the posture — intent upon the frantic murmuring of a tiny tape recorder. He noted that they barely took notice of him: men doing a day's work.

He went into his own office, took a seat beneath a hundred pairs of belligerent eyes staring out of mug shots on the wall; he opened a drawer in the desk and propped up his feet. Delaverne needed time to think, to work out the connection between the dead man and his contacts. Bright red-and-blue bands ringed the tops of his athletic socks, which were bleached to an immaculate whiteness. Beyond them he spotted the quart of Old Grand-Dad: it was early yet.

Comiski's entrance was unexpected, had a curious effect on Delaverne. He experienced a moment of breathlessness: the association faded before he could trace it, added to his irritation.

"What got ahold of you?" he asked.

Comiski took a seat. "Hard times. I fall upon the thorns. Actually, it was the handball court."

"That's an unnatural sport. A man shouldn't be chasing a ball around, down in a hole."

"But it feels so good when you stop."

"Bowling," Delaverne said meaningfully. "Bowling is a natural sport. Now I recommend a nice quiet game of bowling for you members of the news media."

He took out the bottle and a paper cup. Comiski needed a shot, from the looks of him: he was unshaven, bruised, his clothes untidy. Delaverne distrusted men who didn't keep up their appearance; it was a barometer of self- respect and respect for a higher order. Comiski was a good enough drinking companion — a cut above the average media man — and he knew his pro football. But there was something about

94

the way he talked that bothered Delaverne, the sarcasm and the irreverent jokes; he wondered which side Comiski was on.

"I don't want you succumbing in this office," he told him. Comiski accepted the offer of the cup, saluted, drank, and shuddered.

"Most timely and salubrious," he said. "I just dropped by to put you good people on to something. A little guy down at Mary's tried to put some weed on me, and I thought you might want to check him out."

"You're ranging these days, Comiski."

"I was covering the laying of a church cornerstone, when this runt plies me with a vicious drug. So I say to him, 'Littlebit, I'm reporting you to Delaverne, denizen of dope,' whereupon he beats a hasty retreat. I tell you, brother, I was shocked."

Comiski paused to drink. Delaverne glimpsed the light again, lost his brief moment of contentment: he found that he disliked this newspaper reporter. It seemed that the world — the outside — was made up of people pretending to be what they were not.

He said, "You're keeping fine company these days. Were you playing handball with that bunch?"

"Don't tell me you're acquainted with these good citizens?"

"We do get out on the street now and then, can't let you hotshot reporters do all the work."

Comiski crumpled the cup. "Well, I was just checking — making sure the taxpayers get their money's worth." Delaverne groped for the association. The men in the outer office had stopped the tape recorder and sat staring at Comiski; the mimeograph machine rattled on. Suddenly he had it: Parks. Delaverne had often seen them laughing together in Comiski's

95

office; there was a break and entry on a grave out at LaFayette; it was Parks who owned the horse.

Delaverne got up and closed the door; he felt obliged to convince himself.

"What's going on?" he asked.

Comiski smiled, shrugged his heavy shoulders. "You got me there."

"You have any idea who you're messing with? Do you? Tell me who you think has the biggest stake in the racket."

"Which one? A Dallas oilman runs the pinballs, Miami has the heavy hand in the track..."

"I mean my side. Who's really into narcotics?"

"Don't tell me — it's the Polish Mafia!"

"Heh, heh." Delaverne was taking it slow, methodical. "You could call it the Mafia — the Nigra Mafia."

"It's usually the boys on the bottom."

Delaverne opened the door. "You check with the morgue this morning?"

"Not yet. Why?"

"I recommend you check with Gomer."

Comiski went out. Delaverne sat down, stared at the crushed paper cup on the edge of his desk. He longed for the company of clean and unquestionably right-thinking men; instinctively he raised his fingers to the coarse bristles of his mustache. It was the sole adornment of an unremarkable face — lending authority — but maybe it should go. The sight of facial hair on televised news programs had lately made him almost physically sick; it was time for a general reassessment.

Right-thinking men. He had noticed their bumper stickers on the most unlikely cars — a sun rising against a background of deep blue — felt admiration at the society's whispered name: Citizens for a New Tomorrow.

Delaverne felt alone, left out; he picked up the phone and dialed the Vice Squad's extension.

"Give me Bates," he said.

THE MORNING was full of dust. At the end of the street the wrecking ball tore into another tenement, sending tremors of doom through every building left on the block; Carrie decided to walk away from the racket, even though she had to pass the tavern on the corner where stevedores lounged in the doorway, talking up anything that moved.

A cab pulled up beside her. The driver was a Negro, and she was surprised to see a white man in a raincoat get out and move to cut her off; Carrie's hand automatically delved into her purse, feeling for the handle of the broken bread knife. Her parcel from Maison Blanche, tied with string, fell to the pavement.

"Well, well," she said. "Mistah Reportah."

Comiski stooped, retrieved the package. "Where's Tea?" he asked.

"Couldn't say. I'm in a rush, myself."

"Look, it's important. Don't tell me you haven't heard?"

Carrie's eyelids fluttered involuntarily; the backdrop rattled in her head, threatened to come crashing down. Whatever had happened, she didn't want to hear about it.

"Later," she said, pushing past. She climbed into the cab and slammed the door.

Comiski didn't protest; he paid off the driver, leaned into her window.

97

"I've got to find Tea. He's playing very mean games."

"Listen." Carrie allowed herself to look at him: the man's face was a mess; he didn't avoid her eyes, which was strange. She decided he must be some kind of mark. "I need five dollars real bad."

Comiski pulled a handful of crumpled bills from his pocket, flattened one out; Carrie hesitated, then took it. The driver sat hunched over the wheel, watching the proceedings in his mirror.

"Thanks," she said. "Come round later, if you want."

"When?"

"Any ole time. Let's go, man."

The cab pulled away. Carrie didn't want to look back, but going around the corner she did, saw a battered white man standing in the gutter, forlorn and comical — as out of place, she decided, as a spade in a voting booth. Comiski had surprised her with the offer of money; she didn't like that kind of surprise.

She directed the driver to Clarence's cafe, told him to park in the lot next door and wait. She went up the back stairs, could hear Clarence and his woman arguing in the kitchen; through an open doorway she saw a man in a lime-green shirt lying on a mattress, rolling a cigarette. He called out, "Hey dare lil' dahlin'," and she hurried on down the hall.

Light penetrated the whitewashed window at the end of the corridor, where tiny holes had been scratched to afford a peep-show view of the street; Carrie listened carefully at each door, knocked on the last one.

A girl's voice said, "Who?"

"Let me in, child."

The bolt was drawn, and Clarence's teen-age daughter peered out at her; she cradled a baby in one arm, wrapped in a yellow beach towel.

She said, "I been wondrin."

"He all right?" It was a reflex action: Carrie wanted to ask if anyone knew.

"Fine, he jes fine. Good thing dis baby don' hardly never cry, what wid all dem mens scratchin' round all hours."

"What men?"

"All kinds'a mens." The girl shook her head in disbelief. "We got some traffic in dis heah house."

Carrie looked at the baby: it was wide-eyed, serene, an old man's face in spite of the strands of colored wool that had been clumsily tied to strands of gathered hair. The girl expected her to take it, but she didn't, couldn't have said if she was afraid of caring too much or not at all.

"Put these on him," she said, tossing the package onto the bed; she went and sat by the window, pressed her hands between her knees. "Your stuff's there, too."

The girl lay the baby on the mattress, then tore through the wrapping; she inspected the new baby clothes and her jars of cosmetics.

"Nice," she said. "Dat's real nice."

"The Prince wasn't in here?"

"No, suh. I don' study dat man — he crazy."

"That's what they say."

Carrie watched as the baby was changed. The girl held both feet in one hand while she folded the diaper with the other: she was so much better at it than Carrie, whose attentions usually brought on the choking tantrums. She wished the baby would stop staring at her, realized his eyes were drawn by the light.

The girl said, without looking up, "Dis baby look white to me."

Carrie didn't speak; the girl went on with her work.

"What you gon do wit dis baby, then?"

"I'm giving him to welfare."

"Oh, yeah," the girl said.

Carrie closed her eyes. It was no time to sleep: she had to move.

"I'll be needing a bottle, most likely."

"Dat's right."

Carrie took the satchel and then the child, wrapped in the clean white thermal blanket. She waited, felt a rush of gratitude when she realized he wasn't going to cry; she eased to the door.

"You won't say anything?"

"No, suh." The girl sat down on the bed, picked up the jar of Lite 'n Fine. "You tell dem over dare," she said, "take good care of dat baby."

Carrie went down the stairs, picked her way among the broken boards and brick ends littering the lot. The earth trembled under the crane's assault; she covered the child's mouth and nose with the blanket's border. The ancient eyes blinked at the noise and the brightness of the sun; the body lay perfectly still.

She got into the cab, told the driver to take her to the West Bank.

"Go up the River Road," she said. "I'll tell you when."

So she was on her way. If Tea knew he would settle her hash; the funny thing about it was, Tea gave her the idea. If you're looking to see what's there, he said, it's a white baby. For Carrie that was a revelation: the possibility would never have occurred to her, any more than she could have considered herself white — *really* white. All she needed was another birth certificate and a little bread for maneuvering, and he could avoid a special sort of suffering; it was a thing she could do.

Tea once told her that for two hundred dollars a blood could get anything done in Tampa. Carrie took a chance, peddled a fraction of their stash, then found she had to go no farther than a dry cleaners on Basin, where a stuttering albino Negro with peroxided hair sold her a photostat registered in Shelby County, Tennessee. She wanted to give the con a gloss, and she went to the public library on Loyola and borrowed a typewriter, copied from a paperback historical novel a letter written by the posturing heroine to the prospective step-parents of her illegitimate child; the story, she remembered, had something to do with Napoleon.

...I beseech you to give succor to this unfortunate being, in time of turmoil, as I have lately fallen into indigence...

The cab labored up St. Charles, followed the levee, mounted the approach to the Huey P. Long Bridge. Rusted iron hulks lay among the rail lines of the Avondale shipyard, steel skeletons picked clean; derricks shuttled back and forth between the carcasses — spiny scavengers from another world — and men in white helmets clung to the girders like insects.

Carrie held the baby close, gently untied the bits of colored wool and dropped them onto the floor. This was the way it ought to be: traveling quiet and comfortable, out of reach, touching something that was yours, so close to home.

Rows of faded pillbox houses gave way to stands of

pecan and cottonwood, low fields of sugarcane. The smell of woodsmoke, the sight of cotton stalks not yet plowed under, brown and brittle in the autumn sun, reminded her of workers bent double in the moist furnace of a July morning, their clothes a riot of tatters and patchwork, trailing long burlap sacks. She heard the lilting cadence of Cajun and a pidgin English spoken by the real swamp people, felt the bowls' sharp spines against her fingertips. There were good times: a wagon trip to the Plaquemines ferry when she was five, a rally where the politicians served hot sausage and watermelon and lemonade even to the blacks, before once again having themselves elected, the day she decided to leave. The memories stuck; later, shoving synthetic food into the slots of a drafty automat in Chicago or navigating the wind off the lake, she could call up that sun, the darkness heavy and still with heat, the taste of Louisiana Red Hot, and the smell of burning saw grass.

A red mailbox emerged from the tangle of vines at the side of the road; she pointed, and the driver turned into a lane paved with oyster shells and lined with cypress. The raised plantation home at the far end had an incongruous wing built of prefabricated siding and topped with a television aerial; the brick columns were painted white, and a ramp led up to the porch. Faded deck chairs cluttered the spot of lawn hacked out of the surrounding jungle. There wasn't a living thing in sight; Carrie saw a child's swing with a broken dangling seat.

"You wait," she told the driver. He didn't offer to open the door, and she got out with difficulty, afraid that the baby would begin to cry. Carrie went straight up the steps and into the house, stood in the hall, and tried to control her breathing. There was an antiseptic smell about the place; the telephone receiver lay in the midst of printed forms on the desk, and a copy of *Life* magazine beside it had a spot on the cover that appeared to be blood. From the adjacent room came the murmur of conversation and the clatter of dishes.

A muscular woman wearing pink furry slippers with the backs mashed flat shuffled into the hall, picked up the telephone, and told it, "Doctor's at the table. He says there's no hurry, he'll see you after the holidays."

She nodded, replaced the receiver, turned and saw Carrie; her eyes narrowed.

"What is it?"

"I've come," Carrie said, and the words stuck. "I've come with a baby. For adoption."

"You got an appointment?"

"No, I don't reckon I do."

The woman came forward, raised a chapped hand and plucked away the blanket; Carrie waited for the sight of the slack jaw, the watery mastiff's eyes wide with disbelief, but she remained indifferent.

"This here your baby?"

"No," she said. "No, ma'am."

The woman sighed, turned, and shuffled back into the dining room. Carrie wanted to sit down, was afraid of being caught off guard: no telling what might be coming back through that door. The baby watched her, seemed to be waiting for her to lose heart and fold. *I have lately fallen...*

The woman returned, followed by a tall spare man wearing a T-shirt and a linen suit that had once been white; he was completely bald and he wore bifocals, which gave him the eyes of a maniac, in spite of the fact that he was smiling. The pockets of his coat bulged with a stethoscope, a rolled journal, a ring of heavy keys, and a soiled handkerchief.

"I'm Doctor Porteus," he said, wiping his mouth with a paper napkin. "What's the problem?"

"I've brought this baby."

"Have you now?" He gently turned back the blanket. "Yes, that's a baby, all right. Is she yours?"

"It's a he. No, I just brought him along, for a favor."

"I see. This baby belongs to a friend of yours? Perhaps your mistress?"

"That's it," Carrie said. "He belongs to my mistress."

"Well, now."

Doctor Porteus continued to smile. He and the muscular woman stared at her; no one spoke. She knew something had gone wrong, that they were waiting for a signal she was not prepared to give: maybe it was a show of faith — the good bread. Carrie was about to open her purse when she saw a Negro girl in a white apron slip through the door and take up her position behind the others, chewing at her nails. Carrie fought the panic — she hadn't counted on that kind of enemy inside the camp.

"Why did you bring the baby here?" Doctor Porteus asked.

Carrie nodded toward the woman. "I told her."

"Tell me."

"For adoption," she said.

"I wanted you to say it. We can't have people accusing me of planting ideas, can we?" His laughter was desperate. "Well now, if you'll trust the child with Miss Erwin, she can give him the once-over while we talk."

The woman stepped forward, arms extended. Carrie

stiffened: so that was it — she didn't want to believe it just might happen. Carrie looked at Miss Erwin's lantern jaw, her jellied eyes; she wasn't giving her baby to *that*.

"I see." Doctor Porteus turned and said, "Clara!"

The black girl came up, grinning, belying her allegiance; Carrie surrendered the bundle, waited for the outburst. The baby would cry, and she would have an excuse to leave. She glimpsed an alternative to her life — to everyone's life — but couldn't hold on to it: for an instant she saw that things could be different, knew she wouldn't get another chance.

The baby smiled. The black girl cradled it affectionately, followed Miss Erwin down the hall; Doctor Porteus took Carrie by the elbow, led her into his office.

The room was full of shadows, crowded with heavy stuffed furniture claimed by mold; stacks of newspapers and magazines bound with cord lined one wall, and another was covered with volumes the color of old parchment and burgundy. Behind Doctor Porteus's cluttered desk stood a glass case full of dust-laden surgical instruments. The windows were sealed with masking tape and the shades drawn; Carrie detected a new smell, something harsh and disturbing.

"Rest yourself," he said.

They sat down. Doctor Porteus took from his pocket a box of polished cherry bearing the silver intaglio of a fleur-de-lis, flipped it open and thrust thumb and forefinger inside, swiftly applied them to each nostril: it was almost a reflex action, less remarkable than a man blowing his nose. She saw that the top of the desk, the lampshade, the papers and journals were all covered with a thin patina of snuff.

"Wellnow," DoctorPorteussaid. "Tellmewhoreferredyou."

105

"My mistress."

"I'm afraid that won't do."

"I forget, then."

"Your reference — was he black or white?"

"You might say he was both."

"I see. Well, I shouldn't have to tell you that adoption is a vastly complicated procedure, ridden with stumbling blocks and pitfalls and expenses, to say nothing of certain petty governmental jackals..."

"How much expenses?"

"Two hundred dollars' worth."

Carrie took the envelope out of her purse, placed it on the desk.

"There's one hundred and sixty. A certificate and a letter, too. A letter from my mistress. Maybe I can get her to send you the rest."

"I suppose you have power of attorney?"

"I'll get my mistress to send you that, too."

Doctor Porteus opened the envelope and ran his thumb over the edge of the bills, didn't count them. He glanced at the birth certificate and discarded it, unfolded the letter, and read through it twice; Carrie saw him watching her over the rims of his spectacles that shone like polished half moons in the lamplight.

"Not very subtle," he said.

Carrie snatched at the envelope, but Doctor Porteus had her by the wrist: his hand was smooth and cold.

"Do you know what I despise?" he said. "Tell me what you think I most despise."

Carrie felt inside her purse. She was going to cut this white

106

man's fingers off at the knuckles, but before she could get the bread knife out he released her, fell back in his chair.

"I despise that grotesque phenomenon known as the redneck. I despise him even more than you can imagine. Now you won't understand the legacy involved, but you will understand the hate. I don't embrace coloreds as a group, mind you — I have reservations there — but rednecks I abhor, individually and collectively. Have you heard of Bienville?"

Carrie stared at the envelope: she wasn't up to all that jive, needed a boost. What was that smell that seemed to come from Doctor Porteus's snuffbox?

"You mean the street?" she said.

"I mean the man. My family is older than yours, my dear, antedates the Populists by several hundred years. Don't think it was the demise of the Confederacy that brought us down and raised the rednecks to power, because it wasn't — the war was simply a catalyst. The blight set in long before that, when the first sycophantic bailiff begged and grafted enough funds from his beneficent master to buy a hectare of swampland or to set up a soap and candle shop — that was our great mistake, and the origin of their power. Unfortunately we never had an indigenous peasant stock to bolster — a coalition of aristocrat and peasant isn't unheard of, united against the common foe. You people," and he made a sweeping gesture in Carrie's direction, "were the closest thing we ever had. Now you have degenerated and I have degenerated, and they — *they* — have prospered."

Carrie shifted in her chair. No sound came from the hall-way; she wondered if Doctor Porteus had locked the office door. "It's too late to change things," he said. "One can only go through one's personal — perhaps inverted — forms of protest. Once I was determined that I — that is, my milieu — would be heard from. Some symbolic act of defiance resounding enough to be recorded, to remain of at least academic significance — to show that the order has survived, has remained aloof from distinctions of color and money and political persuasion." He leaned toward her. "Do you know that I once considered assassinating Russell Long?"

Carrie said, "About the money..."

"Then I came to the conclusion that one can only resist the *idea* of compromise. One must carry out one's resistance without hope of recognition or even of efficacy within one's lifetime. It's a religious notion, actually — ridiculing and degrading evil. You see, my dear, I hit them where it hurts the most, though they might never know."

The door opened and Miss Erwin looked in, signaled to Doctor Porteus, and withdrew.

"If you'll take the baby," Carrie said, "I'll see about more money..."

"I have already taken him."

The smile was gone; his eyes frightened her.

"You aren't to come here again," he said.

Carrie got up and went out into the hall; she expected Doctor Porteus to follow, but the door closed behind her and she heard the key turn in the lock.

"Hey!" she called. "Shouldn't I sign something?"

There was no answer. Carrie looked around, hoped to find the black girl in the apron, or even Miss Erwin, saw only a very old man rolling his wheelchair like a stiff mechanical toy across the corridor. Suddenly she placed the odor from the snuffbox: once when she sniffed cocaine her nose bled for half an hour and she couldn't escape the clamor of heavy bells. She wondered what Doctor Porteus was hearing.

"Hey," she said softly, waited for her child's cry; she heard nothing but the sound of a television set warming up.

Carrie's eyelids were leaden, oddly sticky; the pull toward sleep was strong. She stepped out onto the porch, shielded her face from the sun, felt her way down the railing to the open door of the taxi.

THE RUINS smoldered in the late afternoon. The street was deserted, littered with trash and bits of glass and shingle; staved-in shop windows were strung together like a row of gutted crypts, the doorways cluttered with empty Mogen David bottles and drifts of cigarette butts. In the background loomed the crane — the mechanical stalker camped for the night — the salient boom resplendent in the sun's last light.

Comiski stood beneath the tenement windows and tried to pick out the girl's room. He couldn't distinguish among the filthy panes; some were marked with a large white X — tracks of the dead encroaching upon the living. He started up. The building might have been empty, except for the trilling of a bass saxophone drifting down the stairwell; he paused on the landing to listen, pulled the pint of Jim Beam from his raincoat pocket and drank. Old home week.

Her door hung open against the latch chain. Comiski could see her lying on the bed, smoking and staring out the window; he was fascinated by her hair — an energized mane that sprang to life with the slightest movement of her head, as if it had guts of its own. She wore no jewelry or makeup, just a thin saffron

109

dress and Woolworth's sandals.

He knocked. She jumped to her feet, switched off the radio, peered out into the hall.

"Oh, yeah," she said, and let him in. "Now what is it, Mistah Comiski?"

"I want to know who hit the jockey. Who murdered Littlebit?"

She stared at him, backed away, sat heavily on the bed. "No," she said. "Oh, shit, man, no!"

"Where's Tea? Where's your brother?"

"Don't come asking me that. Who knows where Tea is? He said he'd be here, but I don't see him, do you?" She fumbled with another cigarette. "They must have gotten spooked — that's it. Those honkie runts were afraid Littlebit might spill things, so they wasted him. Littlebit was very nervous, you know."

"*They* hell! They didn't do it — Tea did."

"And just what makes you say that?"

"Because for obscure reasons he used my razor."

Comiski felt winded; he sat down on the spindly chair, uncapped his bottle.

"There are more conventional methods for getting rid of an employee," he said.

"It's not like that, Paddy — any of them runts can climb onto my horse in Littlebit's place. If Tea did do it, there's other reasons, too. He's got big plans."

"Not long-range ones, I hope. If I know Littlebit's buddies, your brother won't be laboring in this transitory world much longer."

"You don't know Tea's buddies. And he's not my brother,

he's my husband."

"Some domestic scene."

She turned on him. "What do you know about it, white man? Tea and I have been through some shit you wouldn't believe. Now if he did what you say, I'm sorry — sorry for Tea. He just won't give up. Ever."

"That's a very long time, indeed."

Comiski offered her the bottle, took a drink.

"You were a fool to let him lead you over here and then put the touch on you. A fool!"

"I was looking for something," he admitted.

"Well, ain't that romantic? What you mean is, you felt con*cerned*. You mean your great big ole lily-white liberal heart was just a-flopping over with *concern* for us bloods. And ole sugar daddy Parks was a *friend* of yours, right? And the poh-lease ain't *really* your friends, right? And you're really sorry about the times you must have stood around watching the Man crack black men's heads and fuck black girls up one side of the ward and down the other. Right? What you really mean is that you *care*."

She got up and stood before the dressing table, looking at her own reflection.

"I wish I was the one to do it," she said. "I wish I was. But there's some things I can't do. Tea says I don't have a calling."

"Tell me about the big plans."

"You'll be hearing soon enough." She picked up a comb, jerked at her hair, threw it down. "I'm hungry. I'm empty and Tea goddamn his soul won't show till tomorrow night — I just know it. Now what I think is, I think you should take us out for a bite."

She flung open the door, stood defiantly over him with her feet apart, the bright material of her dress pulled tight across her thighs; Comiski worked the bottle back into his pocket.

"Enchanted," he said, and followed her down the stairs and out into the dusk. Black men in overalls came to the open door of the tavern on the corner and watched them, silent and bemused; a hunchbacked woman poking about in the rubble with her cane wheeled and gaped. The girl seemed to notice nothing. She was as much a foreigner as Comiski; he decided they made an appropriate couple.

"You from around here?" he asked.

"Hereabouts — Plaquemines."

"I've heard about Perez and his bunch down there."

"Oh, yeah. Things are like incredible. I picked up enough to get out, four years ago, bought a ticket to Chicago and stood up on that bus all the way from Jackson to Memphis. I carried a cardboard suitcase and a paper bag full of Bunny Bread and collard greens. That's how raw I was. Tea says he's going to waste Perez, when he gets the time."

"Is that part of the big plans?"

"A small part," she said.

They crossed Poydras and stood uncertainly on the corner, at the edge of the white business community; Comiski saw the trolley rattle off down Carondelet and the newspaper offices beyond. The afternoon traffic crept past, and men in suits and ties leaned over their steering wheels, watching them.

"I'm feeling like my usual evening aperitif," the girl said. "I'm feeling like breezing into Maylie's and chatting with all my friends."

Comiski followed her toward the hundred-year-old

wisteria vine that draped the restaurant's portico. He imagined the bankers and the stockbrokers drinking their Southern Comfort and talking soy beans; he was perspiring.

"What's the matter?" she asked him. "You losing heart?"

"It's not my kind of place."

"Stop worrying — I'm black, not you."

She pushed through the doorway.

Comiski silently rejoiced: it was too early for the bankers; a white-haired gentleman with a gold chain across his paunch sat at the far end of the room reading an afternoon newspaper — Comiski's crime report — and he didn't even look up. The bartender stopped peeling lemons and stared at the girl with guileless amazement.

"You git on out of here," he said.

"We want us some drinks." She rested her arm on the rail. "Give me and my friend here some of those martinis."

"I ain't giving you shit."

"Now that's not what I asked for, Cracker."

The man jerked up his sleeves, revealing forearms like boiled hams, leaned over the bar.

"Merle!" he called.

A drawn little man came out of the kitchen, drying his hands on a dishtowel. He wore a wide silk tie emblazoned with a Rebel flag; his shirt pocket was stuffed with pencils.

"What you-all want?" he asked.

"We want some drinks," the girl said. "We want us some great big ole martinis."

"This here's a private club. Now you git!"

"My, my, ain't that nice? Well, we'll just join up in your private club."

Merle turned to the bartender. "She wants to join the club. Ain't that a kick in the ass?"

They laughed dryly. Comiski had an insight: they should all sit down and have a drink — a cooling febrifuge — take up the argument later. He of course would have two drinks...

Merle said, "You don't qualify. Our members have to be eighteen years of age, and they have to be white."

The bartender pushed a stack of heavy glass ashtrays in front of her. Comiski noticed that the white-haired man had spilled his drink over the newspaper, and he was making spastic efforts to stand. His feet appeared to be entangled beneath the chair.

The girl swept the ashtrays off the bar, and they bounced noisily at Merle's feet; two of them shattered.

Comiski pushed her toward the door.

"Why you *nigger*..." Merle said, and he hit Comiski ineffectually on the ear; the bartender came around gripping the neck of a bowling pin. The man with white hair found his voice at last, began to shout.

Comiski walked backward, herding the girl outside; the men followed, watched as he hustled her along Poydras. A car pulled up in front of the restaurant, and the bartender bent over and began to talk urgently with the driver. Comiski thought: how quickly the reaction sets in — the terrible swift sword of retribution. Already he could feel the trouble stirring. Across Loyola the lights in the offices of the Federal Building blinked on like searchlights; the carillon bells lisped through another round of "Danny Boy," mocking in their ethereal imprecision.

"Why did we just do that?" he asked.

She jerked her arm away. "Why not? Maybe I can't touch

the bastards, but I can sure mess up the view — I do that best."

They entered the ruins again; Comiski stepped behind a crumbling brick wall to drink.

"I don't suppose you had to go in there," she said. "I suppose that's something."

She led him across the lot toward a clapboard cafe. One wall was painted red a decade before, bore the inscription, CHAT 'N CHEW, NO. 2; the windows were plastered with cigarette and pomade advertisements.

"You can tell all your friends you tasted soul food," she said.

"What makes you think I'm interested in soul food or in martinis? You're big on extremes."

"And you're big on fence-sitting. The water rat floating down the bayou, culling crap from both banks. Don't come in if you don't want."

The narrow shotgun structure was crowded with makeshift tables and chairs; Christmas lights and strips of tinsel hung from the beams, and a juke box with exposed entrails shuddered through a lugubrious version of "Born to Lose." A veil of smoke drifted out of the pass-through from the kitchen, smelled of fried cornmeal.

A group of black men sat in one corner, drinking beer from quart bottles; the heavyset proprietor got up from his plate of red beans and rice and stepped behind the bar. He smiled benignly.

"Good e'nin. What can I do fo' you-all?"

"What do you want?" Comiski asked her.

"Nuthin.'"

It was a new intonation, a lapse into dialect; he said, "But you told me..."

"I'm not hungry no more. You eat."

Comiski ordered an oyster loaf and a beer; the man disappeared into the kitchen and returned almost immediately, carrying half a loaf of French bread. He set it in front of Comiski and stood watching, his flat glistening face exuding hospitality.

Comiski began to eat, spat bread onto the plate; he opened the sandwich and found the oysters and garlic butter laced with soap powder.

"You eat it," he said.

"Why, we'd be dee-lited."

The man beamed, reached for the plate and upset the glass of beer; he pushed it into Comiski's lap with his towel.

"Why, we's *so* sorry."

Comiski got off the stool, brushed at his trousers. The men in the corner stopped talking; the juke box hummed expectantly.

"Dat'll be fi' dollar," the proprietor said.

He put a one-dollar bill on the bar.

"Now we done tol' you..."

The girl made a cabalistic sign with her left hand, headed for the door; Comiski followed her.

The man called, "We reckon dat'll be 'nuff."

"I'm sorry," she said, when they were on the street. "I didn't figure on that."

They walked toward the expressway; the beer felt cold against the old bruises on Comiski's thighs. He glanced behind them, saw two women talking in a darkened doorway and a man in an orange wig who passed under a streetlight like a somnambulist and vanished in an alley. He thought he heard the echo of a motorcycle.

"You better come up for a while," she said. "You might be marked."

They climbed the stairs in darkness; the room was empty. She switched on the radio, waved him toward the bed.

"Make yourself at home. I'm going to put on the kettle."

Comiski sat down without removing his raincoat, drank, and held the bottle between his knees.

"What's your name?" he asked.

She stood at the stove, her back to him; he could hear her laughing.

"Carrie. What's yours?"

"Andrew." Comiski couldn't remember the last time someone had called him by his first name. "It was a concession to my mother's family. I grew up in Mississippi."

"That's wonderful, Andrew. See if you can find something besides that sorry-ass Muzak."

He tuned in Pete Fountain and his mooning clarinets, had another drink. The girl carried a soup spoon with the handle bent double to the table, unrolled a piece of towel that protected a yellow syringe; she carefully filled it with the liquid in the spoon.

"Some kettle," Comiski said.

"Don't get excited, Andrew. This ain't smack." She held both arms up to the light. "Some people get upset about a little speed. Remember, I never did get that aperitif."

She inserted the needle with careless assurance. Comiski closed his eyes; when he opened them again, he saw three bubbles scuttling up the blue trace inside her biceps like some apparatus in a fish tank.

"Those things are going to take out one side of your heart."

"The AMA puts out that propaganda," she said. "A little air never hurts."

The mass of hair engulfed her face. He turned away as she went through the motions of cleaning up, watched the taillights of speeding cars follow the curve of the expressway and drop from sight.

"You think I'm strung out, Andrew. I'm not strung out — I'm bored."

"I'm going. You tell Tea..."

"Forget Tea," she said. "He's got things on his mind, won't be coming around here."

She sat down on the bed, touched her lips with her tongue; her eyes were bright and aggressive.

"When Tea needs somebody, he gets a hold on them, like when he needed daddy Parks. He needed Parks, see, so we all hooked up — a regular *ménage à trois*. Now Tea doesn't get behind sex anymore, and Parks wasn't much better, at his age. Some *ménage à trois*. Tea says when his plans get underway, then he can ball again. He says it's a matter of priorities."

Comiski said, "Tell me who broke into Parks's grave."

"Don't you know who that was, Andrew? I thought everybody knew that one. It was that same bunch you got messed up with — they were looking for the stash."

"What stash is that?"

"Our smack, Andrew."

"You mean heroin?"

"Wow. I mean smack. Horse, honch, duji, H, snow, heroin — it's all the same animal. Parks kept it hid in a pad with three crazy white people and a whole mess of cats. The honkie runts never could find it. That's how come... "

"That's why they defiled the corpse," he prompted.

"That's it. Just clean honkie fun, stealing black men's heads. They even brought it round for us to look at — friendly persuasion."

Comiski shuddered; Carrie's constant bouncing motion made him seasick.

"It's a shame Parks crumbled before the last drop," she said. "Now all that bread's going into the big plans. You should hear Tea talk about it, Andrew. He's all the time singing about the New Order, some black citadel he says is going to poke up out of the ashes. Shit like that."

"Tea's a poet."

"He's a fanatic." She touched the scab on Comiski's wrist. "Hey, they really leaned on you."

"I'm going." He spoke decisively, could think of no place to go; the bottle was empty.

"Don't do that, Andrew. I couldn't stand sitting round this place on my lonesome. Tea's not coming back, you see, and then my baby..."

"Your baby?"

"Oh, forget that, man. It's just been one of those days, it really has."

Comiski was affected by her palsy. He covered her lips with his hand; the line of her mouth was soft yet precise, moving against his fingers as the words went on. He had a vision of his bare neck pierced by the rusty blade he had noticed in her purse. *What your white man most fears...*

It was a fumbling embrace. The bourbon bottle clattered

119

against the floor; the scent of her hair was feral and disturbing. "Well, well," she said.

Comiski was embarrassed by the sound of crumpled plastic, got up to take off his raincoat; Carrie stripped away the saffron dress and sat bare-chested on the very edge of the mattress, reflecting his own amazement.

TEA SPRINTED across the mall of the housing project and into the center building; he took the steps two at a stride, felt like a schoolboy returning late for supper. It was a new structure compared with the tenement where he stayed, but many of the lights in the hall were broken and there were dark stains in the corners of the landing, a jungle of obscenities and cryptic messages scribbled over the walls. Soul poetry. The place was too familiar: the aroma of baking corn bread, the sound of laughter from an open door cajoled him, and he came down hard against them. After tomorrow the building would have very different associations.

He paused at the second turning, flattened himself against the wall; plaster gathered beneath his fingernails. Something crouched in the shadows — a black woman laboring along the cement floor with bucket and brush, her head wrapped in a bandanna, naked to the waist. Tea saw her flaccid breasts swing with the rhythm of her work, made a whining sound — a radar device sensing danger. Why was she tracking him? She stopped, leaned on the brush until the bristles bent double, held him with an old woman's crazy eyes. He remembered a barrel stave used for punishment, his father's pale blue work shirt bobbing on the line like the transposed torso of someone long gone, the night he went to sleep with a wad of shortbread in his hand and woke up to the scurry of a rat's feet over his forearm. Tea cried out; the oil lamp burned, receded, and he saw his mother hook a thumb under the strap of her slip. The shadows edged closer to the soot-smudged chimney, pounced upon the flame. A man he did not know began to laugh...

Tea forced himself to walk past the woman, but he didn't look at her; climbing the last flight of stairs, he kept one hand on the banister.

The long silhouette of Jupe stood in a doorway at the end of the corridor. Tea stepped into the dark room without acknowledging him; he moved to the window.

"Ain't no 'lectricity," Jupe said, "but they's a telephone."

"Calvin get that stuff together?"

"Dat's what he say. He say meet him at the garage at leben-thuhty."

Tea scanned the courtyard, the symmetrical arrangement of the buildings, the lights along Desire: no problems — he had only to go home and wait. He pressed his elbows to his body, rested his head against the cool pane. Even if she had been his mother, he told himself, it wouldn't change a thing.

THE NOISE was awesome. Comiski dozed, dreamed of parades, the smell of early spring, and the sodden wonder of Fat Tuesday. He was a young man standing on a balcony off Rampart; his shirt sleeves were torn off at the shoulders and his neck muscles failed him every time he raised the beer can to his lips, allowing his head to fall against the ironwork. He tolerated his double vision: two columns of tinseled Mardi Gras floats parted the crowd like snakes navigating the pollen-laden surface of a pond — there were two masks for every reveler and two moons riding above. Strings of colored beads sailed past him, collided with the wall, and disintegrated in a shower of plastic and cheap glass; the night was full of the stench of burning kerosene. Black men in long aprons, white handkerchiefs wrapped about their heads, held the flambeaux high and pranced with their doubles, swinging the flames in unison. The noise of the crowd was sustained, seemed oddly mechanical.

Comiski woke up to the rumble of heavy machinery. He lay rigid, listening to the rattle of steel treads, the resonance of the diesel engine, the snap of cables; he knew if he opened his eyes he would see the wrecking ball hurtling toward the window like a dead polished sun escaped from its slot in the universe. The war of the worlds. The wall of a nearby tenement went down without a fight.

Comiski gazed up into morning light filtered through mortar dust. The hangover was powerful; he pondered the loss of a million brain cells, dead and awash through the wasted vessel of his body. Azam and azack. He could see Carrie's bare back, the soft curve of her hip draped in the folds of blanket; she stirred at the racket of demolition, snored softly on. He wanted to rouse her and lose himself again in the contours of that agitated flesh, the scent of her hair, and the casual assurance of her touch, but something stopped him: it was a new day.

He rolled away from her, caught his breath — he could have reached out and touched Tea. The black man sat hunched forward in the chair, asleep, his head jostled by the passage of each exhausted breath. His arms hung limply between his legs; one hand was wrapped in the black scarf stained with dirt and dried blood.

With graceless stealth Comiski rolled off the mattress, gathered up his clothes. He was too frightened to reason, knew only that he did not want to be murdered in the nude. As he fumbled with garments that seemed conspired to prevent his entrance, light threatened to break through the lattices of his mind — an intimation of the origin of things — and he actually raised a hand heralding the arrival of understanding and solution. The dead cells swarmed, left him half-dressed and gesturing like a soapbox orator lost in dreams.

Tea was watching. His chin rested on his chest, but his eyes were open: he came awake like a bird — unblinking and alert.

"Well, fool," he said. "How you feel?"

Comiski didn't answer; his feet felt very cold.

"I suppose you're feeling mighty proud, I suppose you're just chuckling to your big gray self this morning." Tea stood up. "Do your ole honkie heart good, having it off with a soul sister?"

Comiski wanted to say yes, it did do his heart good. He felt like a truant schoolboy with a genuine and moving explanation for his apparent misconduct, but Tea never allowed him to make it. He lashed him with the back of his hand, filled Comiski's head with a shriek.

Tea told him, "You're going to die, fool. Not now but soon. You think on it."

He went over to the sink, turned on the faucet, and held his hand under the water, began to unwind the scarf.

"Get dressed," he said. "We're going out."

"I'm not going anywhere with you, my good friend."

"You do what I say. The heat would be mighty interested to

find out it's you that owns that razor blade."

"If I may say so, you're out of your mind."

"Am I, Mistah Repohtah? I bet you even went round and told your police friends about Littlebit and his bunch, just to get them off Sis's back." He watched Comiski, made a harsh sound like laughter. "I knew it! I knew she'd bring you round. You told yourself you were helping out a poor little *Knee*-grow chick, when you were really hustling her black ass."

Comiski started for him; Tea slipped his hand into the pocket of his Windbreaker.

"Easy, fool. I don't want to have to waste you before your work's done.

Tea moved across to the bed, pulled the blanket over Carrie's shoulders; he motioned Comiski toward the door, followed him down the stairs and out into the back lot. The sunlight was sudden and intense and offered no revelations. Comiski's dilemma was thrown into stark relief against a clapboard fence, where he saw his shadow being prodded by a smaller one through the residue of civilization; behind them the crane snorted and bullied another edifice into thunderous ruination.

They ducked through a narrow passageway and descended an iron staircase to an abandoned garage. The dirt floor was stained with grease and smelled of gasoline; discarded mufflers and radiators were piled in the comer. Two black men wearing leather jackets stood beneath the skylight, pitching dimes at the wall; they paused and stared at Comiski. Another Negro in a flowered shirt jumped down from the workbench and began to chant, "Goddam-muthafuckin-logslidin-backslappin-sona-bitchin-WHITEMAN!"

124

Tea pushed Comiski into the light.

"I want you all to get acquainted."

One of the black men grunted, "He go'n tell, Prince."

"Shut your mouth! Just look."

"You've got a few names and faces," Comiski said.

"It helps pass the time of day."

Tea jostled the thing in his pocket; Comiski began to sweat. On the workbench lay a battery-powered bullhorn and a wooden crate that had been pried open to reveal a row of glass phials neatly packed in excelsior.

"All right," Tea said, "now you're going to run a little errand for us out at the track. You're going to help the brethren make a certain hookup so we can get us some bread to buy corn pone and spareribs, before we give the rest to City Beautiful."

No one laughed; Comiski said, "You've got the wrong boy."

"I think I got just the right boy — the perfect fool."

"Is the money for the big plans?"

"You're a regular genius," Tea said. "The big plans come off, whether we get the bread or not. Money just makes things easier, gets you credit which you need if you happen to be operating in a sick capitalist system. In fact the big plans are already under way — you might just get a taste this..."

"How come you lettin' on?" one of the men said.

"I told you, *shut!*"

"You're out of date," Comiski said. "Burning down buildings — that's passé."

"Not in this burg. Most everyplace else has had it — Atlanta, even Memphis. The Big Easy's just ten years behind the rest of the world, that's all. You might say it's just too goddamn hot to riot."

Comiski wanted to laugh: Tea the intransigent, commanding a miserable band of insurgents who showed dogged respect for his sophistication and Comiski's whiteness — not exactly the hired and paid revolutionary types. For once he wanted to be lucid and persuasive.

"You'll get people hurt, give the cops an excuse."

"The Man don't need an excuse." Tea took a phial from his pocket, ran his thumb along the surface of the glass. "You're right about riots being passé — we're just staging one for openers. We've got to wake up the black people around here."

"What about Carrie? You waking her up, too?"

Tea stepped forward, raised the phial. "First names yet. Ain't that sweet? If you're worried about Sis, fool, be sure you're under that board tomorrow. Be sure you're there right after that sorry-ass horse of hers runs, for both your sakes."

"That horse won't be running — you killed the jockey, remember?"

The man in the flowered shirt shifted uneasily; Tea said, "That'll take care of itself."

"Tell me one thing," Comiski said. "If you're such a revolutionary hero, why don't you go off and do something on your own? Work out your own private grievances and let the rest of us be."

Tea looked at him with interest. "And how would I do that?"

"Retaliate in kind — assassinate somebody whose ideas are radically and actively opposed to your own. Fair play and all that. The rules of the game."

"Decadent bourgeois individualism," Tea said. "You're the one that's passé, man. The rules of the game my ass. You made those rules, we weren't consulted. Do you think it makes any difference to me if the Grand Dragon of the Klan dies or if you die? I don't favor one white over another." He turned to the others. "We're moving."

The man in the flowered shirt replaced the lid on the wooden box, tapped it delicately with the heel of his hand, and wrapped it in a blanket. They started up the stairs;

Tea carried the bullhorn like an aspiring politician on the way to a rally.

"You're a fanatic," Comiski called.

Tea looked back at him. "One more thing — Sis is your contact at the track. Now I know you wouldn't leave poor 'Carrie' standing there, holding the bundle."

Comiski leaned against the bench. He couldn't go back to the tenement, where Tea was probably headed: there seemed to be nowhere, nothing else. For a long time he stood listening to the muffled impact of the wrecking ball. Finally he went up into the sunlight.

CARRIE pushed the suitcase down the last flight of stairs. It came to rest in the shadow of the open door, and she sat down on it to wait, hugged the plastic shopping bag. All that stuff. If the Man dropped around, she was finished; Tea had no right to put the burden on her. She would tell him so, when he came to take her away.

Sleep seemed to cling to her. The street was empty, desolate in the afternoon sun; she closed her eyes, listened to the measured blows of a black man's hammer drifting down the stairwell. A workman in a steel helmet woke her up to say that her tenement was next, began to nail shut the doors of empty rooms, before tearing them down. Carrie couldn't figure that one out. She dressed and then realized Comiski was gone, remembered he was there. If Tea knew...

She didn't want to cripple Tea, would like to wake him up to the fact that she was still around — Carrie wanted him to *look* at her. No big thing. Comiski was just something that happened: not right but not all wrong. Shades of gray. That was funny, could even make Tea laugh if he would stop his hustling and his sweating. It was his method: a jab, a change of stance, another jab — no time to think, no quarter. Then something strange happens. But what? She was afraid; her version was too severe, involved an element of risk even Tea wouldn't dare.

Maybe the stuff did things to her mind, like Tea said. If he knew, he would waste her; if he didn't act, then she didn't matter. All this for nothing. Pulling tight for so long for nothing.

Tea would never leave her maimed: she knew that if she knew anything.

COMISKI picked up the office phone and called the city desk.

"This is your man at the cop house," he told Darrow. "I'm quitting."

"You're what?" It was the first time he had ever caught Darrow off guard. "You can't quit, Comiski. You never got started!"

"Call it a leave of absence," Comiski said. "Whatever you call it, I'm leaving your employ."

"Now why would you want to do that?"

"To write my memoirs. To search for the hairy frog of the Cameroons."

Darrow told someone in the background, "He's stoned." Comiski hung up. He sat down at the teletype machine and began to rap out his final crime report:

The Crescent City was honored today as the recipient of a bona fide riot. This long-awaited event, with all its pomp and pageantry, was sponsored by several Elements, including the Commies, the Northern Yankee Agitators, the Winos, the Lawless-and-Orderless, the Latins, and the Welfare Spongers. The riot was organized by the time-honored Nigra Conspiracy, made up of the Hired and Paid Revolutionary Types famed in story and legend.

A colorful Armageddon was staged along Prytania Street; traffic passed freely.

The Garden District trembled as thousands of bare feet thundered along brick walkways. Statues could clearly be heard tumbling into patio pools. This reporter saw magnolia blossoms plucked at random by the quaint tatterdemalion army.

On the lawn of one prominent home, a servant (cook, Negro) was observed fending off the gay rioters with a wooden spoon, while hymning "Abide with Me"...

Comiski lost his inspiration. He went and stretched out on the couch, covered his face with one arm, ignored the ringing telephone.

JUPE LIMPED across the dirt mall of the project. He wore bright red coveralls; every few steps he paused and pulled at something beneath his trouser leg, looked over his shoulder. Tea kept to the shadow of the passageway, watched his harried progress — a demented cripple pursued by phantoms. Jupe and the other two were all he had; they were just enough.

Tea's impatience had reached a crisis state. He pressed his

129

shoulders against the brick wall, to stop the trembling. Get on, man — *move!* The cool touch of the glass phials in each pocket was an affirmation, the substance of his dreams — the real thing: his only fear was that some unforeseen event, a natural cataclysm or some malicious historical force, would prevent the day unfolding as he planned.

Jupe limped into the passageway. His eyes appeared to be all whites; his rubbery lower lip hung slack.

"Tape won' hol'," he panted.

The greasy leather strap dangled from beneath his trousers — a miserable attempt at arms smuggling. That was the extent to which Calvin was willing to help out: one carbine, fifty rounds of ammunition, and an egg crate full of incendiary bombs put together in somebody's basement. Tea wondered if they worked at all. The equipment was no more than an incitement to vandalism, a mandate for them to pursue their own destruction. Calvin would get his, along with the others on the fringe: given time, Tea would make them all feel a special sort of repentance.

"Where're your brothers?" he asked.

Jupe looked over his shoulder; the habitual shuffle was hampered by the hidden weapon.

"Hold still!" Tea said. "Now you answer me."

"I reckon dey's gone, Prince."

"Gone?" He felt his breath draining away; he pushed away from the wall. "You mean they cut and run?"

"I reckon dey was scar't."

Tea closed his eyes, fought the rage and frustration: yes, they would be getting theirs, all right, but first things first. He revised, retrenched; the day was going ahead.

He said, "That means you got to make the incident."

Jupe rolled his eyes. "I reckon I's scar't, too."

Tea slapped at that big bobbing head. "Why you're nothing but a *nigger,*" he hissed.

"You right, Prince. You sho right 'bout dat."

Jupe's dangling arms jerked spastically. The carbine escaped its binding; the muzzle drove into the dust. Tea cursed long and bitterly.

"All right," he said finally. "You take the piece up. Call the district station and tell them to send a car. From then on things go as planned."

"What I gwine tell dem poh-lease, Prince?"

"Don't matter. Tell them two bloods fighting. Anything."

Jupe hesitated; tears coursed down the vast black cheeks. "I sho hope you be all right," he stammered. "You sho is a man, Prince..."

"Get on now!"

Tea watched him hobble away, for a moment relented: Jupe and the woman who sold hair straightener were the innocents; he could never touch them. The mental index card printed with the solution to his dilemma was still missing. He had no idea how to keep the struggle alive, once the detonator blew, was forced to carry the problem into the field and solve it in real terms; his army was reduced by two-thirds, and the battle not yet begun. *Work out your own private grievances...* It had come to that, after all. Isolated, he might act for all black people: by overreaching, he was going to achieve something brave and new.

Tea sensed the dawning of another maxim: Desperation derives from extremity, if every black could be made aware of his uniqueness — his extremity — then the consequences of action would seem far less terrible than those of non-action. He wished he hadn't left his notebook with Carrie, searched his pockets for something to write on, touched the glass phial, and checked himself. It was the taint again: the white man's reasoning. What were the use of effete abstractions, faced with the memory of his father's death? *Jump boy, jump!* He hated his father for obeying, for being unequal even to ritual protest. Resist or share the guilt.

A black woman in hair curlers walked toward him along the passageway, dangling a naked child by one arm above the carpet of spilled garbage. She glanced suspiciously at Tea, and started up the steps; he waited until she thrust her head over the balcony — an automaton powered by a white's concepts of beauty and propriety. It's happening, Tea wanted to shout. It's happening now!

Black men carrying lunch pails and toolboxes were returning from work, walking along the broken concrete strips that strung the buildings of the project together; Tea felt them register the phenomenon of his unstraightened hair, his scars. Mutilation equals alienation: he was a pariah among his own people. Loneliness was dangerous, weakened his resolution. He might have given the whole thing up, if he hadn't already committed his first act of consequence; the white jockey served more than one end — provided him with influence over another white man and, more important, a terrible sense of accomplishment. That night in the alley Tea felt something rush out of him: it was an unburdening, a release from the rigors of his scheduling, a task actually and irrevocably completed. Then the anxiety returned, more obsessive than ever.

He suspected that he had served Littlebit's ends more than his own: his little body actually seemed to welcome the blade.

Tea's shoulders were trembling again. He sat down on a slab of concrete, in view of the street, hugged his knees. Black children played in the sea of dust in the center of the mall, their calls spontaneous and oddly carefree; he watched them with longing. They were beautiful — the perfect soldiers. Was it a kind of love he felt, when he would have sacrificed any one of them for his ends? Resist or share the guilt. He thought of their — his — child, experienced the merest flutter of regret; he had seen it only once, incubating behind plate glass in the Charity maternity ward — a tiny convulsed gland that could not be construed as black. His embarrassment was equal to his anger: he couldn't escape the notion that his son might grow up to pose for a Silky Smooth advertisement. *Belongs to welfare.* He wondered what Carrie had done with the child.

Tea's brain seemed to heat and expand, without the benefit of his habitual memory. Instead he recalled the scene in the tenement — framed in a vermilion hue — saw Carrie and Comiski lying unconscious on the mattress. So close: never had he exercised such control; his reasoning was swift and decisive and defeating. Killing them at that moment would have been the supreme indulgence: they had greater ends to serve. Later Tea would waste the white man without hesitation; his death was an imminent historical certainty, unworthy of speculation. And Carrie no longer mattered. Her apostasy rendered her dead in life — an unreality.

A squad car cruised across the intersection of Desire and entered the project. Tea watched as it pulled up to the curb next to a group of teen-agers; a white cop got out, stood talking with his hands on his hips, stomach thrust forward. So Jupe was good for something. Tea would need him when the money came - an alter ego and a conscience. The others urged him to hold off until after the delivery, when they could afford all the guns they needed; Tea rejected that sort of dependence. There was more to it — something degrading, something he feared. He looked at his worn shoes and clothes, tasted the residue of cheap food: it had been a long haul — Tea was afraid of all that money.

He stood up. He was no longer shaking; the real thing might even be an anticlimax. He looked at the children once more, remembered a sodden New Orleans winter when he and every black child he knew received roller skates from Santa Claus, because they were inexpensive and indestructible and white men came around in covered trucks, offering them for sale at cut rates. He heard the hundreds of wheels clattering along Dryades Street on Christmas morning, saw a million, ten million, fifty million black souls coasting on skates down a vast concrete incline and into a citadel with walls of burnished brass and sheets of ebony. The army was silent, but there was joy in the thunder of the wheels. The sun blazed black, but cast a definitive light, obliterating shadow; the air was thick with the smell of burning...

Tea slipped his hands into his pockets, walked quickly toward the squad car.

THE CAB swung through a hazardous U-turn directly beneath the traffic light and bounced up onto the curb, making way for the shrieking paddy wagon that crossed the intersection against the red and sped on toward the concrete edifices of the

Desire Street project. Black men ran along the pavements — spectators hurrying to a fire — exhorted by the clarion of the ladder truck; there was no sign of smoke on the low serrated horizon.

"Git out or go with me," the cabbie told Comiski. "I ain't hanging round Niggertown this afternoon."

Comiski got out. The air was full of the antiphony of half a dozen sirens and a faint acrid smell; the packed dirt basketball courts across Desire were deserted, and Negro boys in gym shorts and torn-off Levi's trotted across the field, calling out to one another. He followed the high metal fence, searched the tops of the identical structures for some sign of fire. Black people leaned out of windows, watching the action below; the crowd in the street parted to let the ladder truck through, and firemen in hard hats and short canvas jackets jumped clear, began unpacking lengths of metal tubing.

The grassless expanse in the center of the project was deserted, cordoned off by a score of policemen wearing motorcycle helmets and armed with sawed-off Winchester pump shotguns. A single tear gas canister lay smoldering at the edge of the walkway; three men gripping the ugly blunt launchers stood scanning the windows of the nearest building, searching for a target. Tenants poured out of the complex, filed into the street, talking and gesturing; above the din and the constant wail of sirens, Comiski heard the thick bellicose voice of Tea, amplified by the bullhorn.

"Black men, get guns. Kill the white fools."

His words echoed weirdly among the buildings, and cops and spectators alike craned their necks, trying to spot the offender. Someone gave a mock cheer; people were laughing.

135

Cautiously Comiski pushed through the crowd. An abandoned squad car sat at an odd angle to the street, two wheels resting on the sidewalk: the windshield was smashed, scorched by flames, and sprayed with a white gelatinous foam. The front seat was strewn with broken glass and the empty casings of .38-caliber bullets.

He skirted the car, attempted to cross the sidewalk to the mall; a policeman challenged him, and Comiski took out his press card.

"Git back," the cop said, pressing the stock of his scatter gun against Comiski's chest.

"But I'm with the news media."

"I said git back!"

The cop shoved him roughly down the escarpment; Comiski bowed, edged back into the crowd. Overreaction, that was the word. He noticed that the man was still watching him.

Patrol wagons arrived simultaneously at each end of the block, disgorged bands of men wearing khaki uniforms and shiny baby-blue helmets and armed with long truncheons used by the mounted police. Comiski didn't recognize the force, watched as they moved in ragged formation toward the corner apartment building and out of sight. A contingent of plainclothes detectives trotted past, and Comiski fell into step beside them, headed for the parking lot behind the project. A rookie with glossy slicked-back hair, an eager grin, and the stride of a high school athlete told him, "We re going to kill that sonofabitch."

"I don't doubt it," Comiski said.

"This here's my first riot."

136

"Mine, too. What's going on?"

"Some nigger," he said meaningfully. "He up and bombed that unit."

"Anybody hurt?"

"Not yet. You Vice or Special Squad?"

"Special Squad, that's me."

Comiski saluted, moved off between the buildings. Above him windows were slammed shut, shades and curtains drawn; bicycles and skates lay abandoned in the narrow dirt yards. An old man in his undershorts crept out of a service entrance and, seeing Comiski, dropped his plastic pail of garbage and scurried back inside, locking the door behind him. Tea's omnipotent voice echoed throughout the project: *"Black men get guns. Get your guns now! Kill all white foowoowools."*

A section of the mall burst into flames. It was too spectacular: for an instant Comiski managed to disbelieve it. Two cops dropped their weapons and fled; there was a clatter of shotgun fire, punctuated by the heavy thumping reports of the tear gas launchers. He saw a canister bounce off the wall beside a curtained window and fall back to earth, trailing what appeared to be dirty steam mixed with the oily smoke from the fire bomb. A feeble cry went up from the crowd.

Comiski stepped into a deserted doorway. A Negro in bright red overalls was running along the base of the adjacent building, clawing at the air in front of him, lifting his knees in a fast hurtler's pace: it was one of Tea's revolutionaries — the tall lanky man who had cursed him. Comiski watched him duck into a passageway and tear off the overalls, revealing his flowered shirt beneath. A wedge of policemen sprinted around the corner from which he had come, bristling with revolvers and batons; the black man stepped out and walked toward them, flattened himself against the building and pointed to the passageway. The cops ran past and entered the passageway, emerged carrying the red overalls; they looked up and down the yard for the vanished Negro. Then they started across in Comiski's direction. He stepped back, waited for them to pass. His head ached and his mouth was dry; Tea's voice admonished him: *"White men fuck black girls. Kill the Man. Kill him nowowow..."*

Comiski went for the first sound he heard. There were no faces in the windows now; occasionally black people ran from the doorways along the edge of the mall toward the street and the apparent safety of the crowd. A reinforced corps of policemen with scatter guns advanced in a line and surrounded the main building, held back out of range of the fire bombs. Comiski wondered if Tea had a gun, watched two cops with high-powered rifles crouch and scan the windows through their telescopic sights. The smell of tear gas was nauseating; the sirens never ceased.

A wedge of policemen advanced on the building at a mincing trot. The concrete steps were engulfed in flames, and they fell back in disorder, covering their faces with their arms; the men with the rifles fired indiscriminately, the slugs ricocheting off the building's facade and whining overhead. A tear gas canister smashed a window on the third floor; a woman screamed. Comiski looked behind him, saw a solid wall of blue shirts as policemen herded people into the street and up against the cyclone fence on the other side.

Tea's plea was edged with hysteria: *"Kill them! Kill the whites! Help me kill thememem..."*

138

Comiski scanned the checkerboard of windows: Tea could have been anywhere. He saw one of the sharpshooters put three bullets through a flapping yellow curtain, decided to keep moving. He kept behind the cordon of police, circled the building, and walked into a clutch of men in khaki and baby-blue helmets concealed behind the shrubbery at the edge of the parking lot. They were searching three Negro youths who had their hands against the brick wall; one of the cops was methodically puncturing the tires of an old Cadillac with an ice pick. Another came up to Comiski, twisting the baton in his fists as if it were a huge pepper grinder.

Comiski said jovially, "So these are the ones," and gestured toward the blacks.

"Which ones is that?"

"The troublemakers."

"They're all troublemakers."

He didn't dispute. Handcuffs were attached to the Negroes' ankles; the cops took the chains in hand and jerked them backward, dumping the men in the gravel. Comiski recognized none of the cops. Their uniforms resembled those of the auxiliary police, were identified only by a gold-plated brooch engraved with a rising sun, without names or numerals; they carried only handcuffs and batons, and their mood of aimless belligerency suggested raw recruits.

The man with the ice pick punctured the last tire, sat down on the car fender, and began to roll a cigarette.

Comiski recognized the symptom, placed the faces: they were white trusties from Parish Prison — inmates.

One of them asked Comiski, "What you want, anyway?"

"I'm just reconnoitering."

"You ain't with the Commonist press?"

"Certainly not. I'm Special Squad."

"That's funny — so are we."

They conferred, and Comiski started back in the direction from which he came; one of the men ordered him to stop, but he kept walking.

The siege had moved to the adjacent building. Through the haze of tear gas he could see two policemen with dogs on leashes moving precariously along the ledge of the roof; they met and eased back out of sight. Tea's shrill voice harangued the crowd: *"Kill them! Help me! Help me nowowow..."*

A group of policemen broke from the ranks and stormed the main entrance; they pushed and shoved, fell frantically through the doorway, just as a missile came arching out of a window on the top floor. Comiski recognized the wooden crate trailing excelsior, sunlight glinting off particles of glass, shielded his face against the explosion. He was buffeted by a hot wind; a column of orange flame shot up half the height of the building, with feelers of fire streaking along the ground and scattering the police. A great sigh went up from the crowd. The sharpshooters blazed away, followed by the heavy *thumpthumpthump* of the tear gas launchers; smoke poured from half a dozen windows.

The men with scatter guns skirted the fire and flooded the entrance, pushed through. Comiski watched the window from which the crate had been thrown, waited for Tea's next message, but it never came. He wanted to act, to stop the slaughter: for an instant he envisioned himself the divine mediator, descending on a brocade dais between the belligerents, dispensing goodwill with justice. *Deus ex machina.*

A police lieutenant brushed past Comiski, waving his arms and shouting at the sharpshooters. Somewhere inside the building a semi-automatic weapon fired steadily until it was empty; during the silence that followed he heard a car horn blowing far down Desire. The room on the top floor filled with light. There was a muffled explosion, and the window frame leapt outward, disintegrated in midair; hundreds of shotgun pellets rained against the panes of glass in the building opposite.

At last smoke began to pour from the gutted cavity of Tea's stronghold; a policeman wearing a gas mask leaned out of the window and waved to the men below.

Comiski was running toward the street. There was something in the air more sinister than teargas: short hysterical shrieks, like those of an air raid siren. The department's special riot van crept through the crowd, the metal siding bright in the afternoon sun, and black people swarmed about it, peered through the bulletproof plate glass at the uniformed men sitting in swivel chairs, gripping microphones; the lone figure in the glass turret wore a curious helmet festooned with wires, turning slowly from side to side as he mouthed into a hose-like device.Twice the van was forced to stop while firemen riding the running boards down and propped up power lines with aluminum poles, permitting the turret to pass underneath. The van pulled up onto the pavement beyond the burned out squad car, tottering dangerously, and threatened to crush a score of people who screamed and fought to get away. The siren trailed off, replaced by the steady hum of the air conditioning unit mounted above the cab. A telescopic ariel projected into the air.

Comiski didn't attempt to cross the narrow space

separating the police from the crowd. The fence in the gate across the fence had been chained shut, and cops patrolled the other side, pounding the knuckles of anyone who tried to climb over. Three-wheel motorcycles puttered along behind the line of blue shirts, while the drivers threw down gas masks. The ladder truck was backed out and parked at a right angle to the far end of the fence; behind the truck, Comiski could see a large contingent of baby-blue helmets. The clamor of the crowd increased.

He crossed the mall. Policemen ran past to join the cordon, and a station wagon from the coroner's office bumped over the rough ground and strips of broken concrete, bound for the smoldering building; the driver — one of Gomer's cretins — appeared to be singing. The air vibrated with the amplified static, and a loud determined voice: *"You people will now disperse. You people..."* The words were lost in another metallic shriek; the crowd cheered.

Comiski went around the building at the edge of the project, hoping to get out at that end of the street. Fifty men in khaki and baby-blue helmets were concealed behind the wall; the man stationed at the corner, in view of the riot van, carried a short-wave radio. A Negro in a red vest came around the far side and stumbled into the ranks of the Special Squad, went down beneath a forest of batons. A line of squad cars and paddy wagons stretched to the intersection, where a barricade had been set up; Comiski could see the yellow slickers of a pair of traffic cops waving the cars past.

There was no way out. He might have gotten through at the back of the project, behind the tear gas and dense oily smoke and the bands of roving policemen with scatter guns: he was

142

white and they would probably let him pass. But something held him — Comiski couldn't believe they were actually going through with it.

He returned to the mall. Almost all of the cops in the cordon wore gas masks; the ones without them moved warily along the line, getting upwind from the tear gas launchers. Beyond the ladder truck a group of Specials was turning back a carload of television reporters. Comiski recognized the photographer from his newspaper creeping along the far side of the fence. He raised the camera above his head and fired the flash; a cop walked up and clubbed him in the shins, waited until he fell against the steel mesh, and then hit him at the base of the neck. The cop carried the camera off under his arm, like a football.

The loud-speaker mounted on the riot van warmed and sputtered; the same determined voice: *"You people will now disperse. You will be given a count of ten in which to disperse."*

Comiski grabbed the shoulder of a policeman in the line, tried to explain that there was nowhere to disperse to. It was the same cop who had pushed him down the escarpment, and he smiled grimly while a girl's face was jammed against his belt buckle by the force of the crowd. Comiski tore off his epaulet; the cop looked at him with loathing, didn't turn around.

"One. Two. Three. Four..."

The voice was drowned out by yet another metallic shriek. A cheer went up from the crowd; Comiski was horrified to see that people were laughing.

The police rushed forward, chopping vertically with their clubs: the initial impact sounded like ragged applause. The screams and the shuffling of feet on the pavement was deafening. The crowd surged against the riot van, rocked it dangerously, assaulted the fence; cadres of police launched brief furious expeditions, cutting down people on all sides, fell back to regroup. The heavy percussion of exploding canisters brought panic, and the crowd split in half, rushed each end of the block. Firemen braced themselves behind their long metal poles, backed by the Specials and the ladder truck; the crowd was outflanked on the other side by more men in baby-blue helmets who poured into the street with a sustained Rebel yell, swinging their truncheons like baseball bats. The police cordon was forced back up the escarpment. Black men broke through their ranks and dashed across the mall; dogs trailing bright steel leashes streaked after them.

Comiski received a blow between the shoulders, went down on his hands and knees: he could see nothing but shoes, many of them without owners. A man fell in front of him, smoke pouring from a tear in the back of his coat. People stepped on Comiski's fingers, but he didn't mind; the gas attacked his eyes, enraged him. He tried to stand, but couldn't. The screaming reached a peak, and the earth shuddered; he saw the riot van lying on one side like some bloated prehistoric beast, surrounded by the dark stain of spilled gasoline. The inert body of a woman lay beneath a slab of bulletproof glass; her hand gripped the neck of a broken soft drink bottle.

The pressure shifted, and Comiski stood, was swept across the street. A section of the fence gave way; people flooded through the breach, shrieking and flailing with their arms. The cops on the other side formed a gauntlet and began to club them, and Comiski saw a stumpy policeman with a hairline mustache mark him as a victim. It was the same man who

144

clubbed the photographer; Comiski decided to kill him — a gesture. Tears were running down into his mouth; the crowd heaved violently from side to side. When he reached the fence he saw the cop sitting in the grass, one hand over his face, blood trickling between his blunt fingers and down into the cuff of his shirt.

Comiski fell forward again, crawled along the fence. Black bodies were mashed against the wire a few feet to his right: he could see the mesh cutting into arms and legs and faces under pressure from the crowd. The occasional report of a snapping bone punctuated the overlay of screams, differed from the sound of cartilage splattering beneath polished wood — a fine distinction. His path was blocked by a man in khaki down on his knees, jabbing the broken end of his club through the fence. Comiski crawled around him, thought better of it; he picked up the man's helmet and bludgeoned him behind the ear. He turned and looked at Comiski as if he were a betrayer; the fence split neatly and the man went down beneath a jungle of human feet.

Comiski crawled on. The crowd began to thin out; he saw another member of the Specials straddling the fence, slumped forward with his arms and legs dangling on either side, while three Negro boys in gym shorts beat him with boards, like an old rug. Comiski altered his course, stood, and made for the basketball courts. The paddy wagons and squad cars moved forward, sirens warming up; he looked back and saw clouds of tear gas sweeping the mall, which was littered with bits of clothing, and a group of firemen surrounding the riot van, assisting the dispatchers out through the broken window. Police reinforcements herded groups of black people along the pavements, toward the paddy wagons, striking down the resisters. Two more sections of fence collapsed and the refugees tumbled into the field in legion, scattering the remaining guards.

Comiski's eyes were streaming and his chest ached as he ran out into the intersection. A crowd of unaffected blacks stood on the opposite curb, watching the police vehicles come and go: the violence hadn't reached them.

The cops standing behind the barricade shouted for Comiski to stop, but he pushed through the bystanders and ran on.

DELAVERNE sat alone in his office. The lamp was out; beneath the locked door leading to the outer office seeped the glow of the interrogation light and the frantic lisping of the short-wave, jammed with the appeals of field units fighting for the wire. He didn't like the pitch of the dispatcher's voice: twice he had used obscenity — Delaverne would have to report him. The forces of insurrection must be dealt with by men seasoned in the ovens of experience, without need of common expletives. A good police officer must be the preserver and the purveyor of all that's worthy in a civilization; only he knew the real meaning of order. Delaverne reviewed the survey course of history he had taken at night school, conjured up a vision of Imperial Rome and legions of gleaming centurions' helmets: there was a great and orderly civilization — master of the world and refuge of the Law — undermined in the end by barbarians. Asiatic freaks.

The vision was spoiled by the fact of the Crucifixion; his mind vaulted in panic across nineteen centuries, to the time he began laboring in the interest of universal order. While Delaverne was fighting Japs in the Pacific, Hitler was on the other side of the world killing Jews and Russians. And yet they themselves were enemies. Why? He put the blame on the men in power — the liberal politicians and the bureaucrats and the heads of foundations — the upper strata, untouched by reality, lethal in its permissive ignorance.

For an hour Delaverne had been sitting in the dark, his Smith and Wesson tucked snugly into his left armpit, his hat on his head, waiting for inspiration. At least two of his men would be out there on the street, engaged in extramural activities for which they wouldn't claim overtime pay; his place was beside them and the other Citizens, dealing with the insurgents. But he couldn't bring himself to leave the confines of his office. It had nothing to do with fear: he was simply reluctant to place himself in a position where he might have to kill another human being. A moral consideration. Dealing with narcotics offenders was another situation entirely — a game with established rules, part of a day's work. But Delaverne was not authorized to combat rioters. The argument was irrefutable; actually, he marveled at the hesitation — his weakness — which rendered him an outsider, a titular member of two police forces and loyal to neither.

He picked up the telephone, waited patiently for the switchboard to find him a line, dialed the familiar number. The ringing at the other end took too long; at last he heard his wife's anxious voice.

"What is it?"

"You all right." It was a statement of fact, rather than a question.

"The TV hadn't told me a thing," she said.

"Turn off that set. You want some freak to see the light?"

"But what's happening?"

"Niggers," Delaverne said. "Niggers are what's happening. Now if you hear somebody run across the porch, you go on in the bathroom and lock the door, you hear?"

"I don't like it one bit. You coming home?"

"*Home?*" he scoffed. "How can I come home? I'm needed here. You just stay put and I'll be along later."

He hung up. She was safe enough; Delaverne was thankful there were no children in the house — barrenness could be a blessing.

Over the short-wave came a call for assistance in the neighborhood of Shakespear Park: another sixty-four on a liquor dealer. It sounded like the riot was spreading. He imagined a mass of blacks sweeping through the streets, the torches illuminating wild eyes and white teeth while the bearers danced impertinently; he was most angered by the possibility that they might be enjoying their desecration.

Delaverne said aloud, "Cut the sonofabitches in half."

Still he didn't move.

No LIGHT in the tenement. Comiski ran his hand over broken plaster and strips of board, encountered no switch; his fingers probed empty space, retreated as if he had touched a live wire. That smell — was it grease gone solid in a pan or the ordure of rodents? — seemed stronger in the dark.

He eased along the landing, mounted the staircase. Living things scrabbled inside the walls, emitted frantic little shrieks; the darkness was so charged he could almost taste it. He felt as if he were climbing inside a sealed drainpipe, pressing into hidden debris that would trap and suffocate him. On the top landing he felt his way along the banister, until he judged he was opposite Carrie's room, then stretched out his arms and stepped forward. The door was there, and he knocked, the sound echoing along the black emptiness of the corridor. He considered lighting a match, found that he preferred not to see. The door was unlocked but wouldn't open; he felt along the jamb until he touched the cold studs of three-penny nails that sealed the room like a tomb.

Comiski rested his head against the wood. Soon the confines of that room would cease to exist: the miserable box in which they made love — thirty feet above the ground — would be nothing but an abstract notion hanging in space. A linear memory, like a theorem in geometry. He felt strangely exposed.

Comiski started back for the steps, ran one hand along the wall. He sensed something — movement, an incongruous smell, the sound of breathing — then he touched a face.

Gasping, he fell backward, and the banister broke, sagged out over the stairwell; the supports held, and he clawed his way along them, collided with the wall at the end of the corridor. One of the supports had come loose in his hand, and he thrust it defensively in front of him.

He heard nothing; then a voice said, "Wheah is she, Dude?"

The bastards! he thought. The grubby little bastards! His head throbbed, and he felt nauseous and afraid: he wasn't going down for them again.

"We figger yew know best," said Hoppy. "We don't care if

149

yew want to knock off a little black tail, Dude — git yew a little poontang. We ain't prejudiced. Hit's that other stuff we want."

Comiski heard their boots inching along the floor, the minute jangle of steel. He slid his shoulders across to the other wall, crouched and gripped the stave with both hands — a switch hitter's ready stance.

"Now yew 'n us ain't got no fite, Dude. Yew help us git that stuff, then we can all sit back 'n watch the coons and the fuzz cut one another down. Maybe yew ain't heard, Dude — there's a revo-lew-shun goin' on."

The voice drove him berserk. Comiski took a step forward and swung, leaning into the blow; he connected with something solid, heard a low moan as the body fell away. In the scramble that followed a chain grazed his head and wrenched out a few precious hairs, and the sleeve of his raincoat was torn. He held the stave by both ends and rushed forward; another body went down, and a voice very close to him shouted, "Watch that fan!"

Comiski tumbled down the stairs. An explosion followed the flash of light; the plaster next to his head disintegrated, stinging his eyes and face. He was on his back, paddling wildly. That one gunshot was the ugliest sound he ever heard: he imagined a mail-order pistol fitted with a homemade silencer and dumdum bullets filed flat across the noses and nicked with crosses for luck. He hit the floor at a sprint, flung himself through the door. During the instant he was framed against the light from the street he expected to hear that sound again, but he heard nothing at all.

The night air was cool and damp. There wasn't a cab in sight; he ran toward Poydras, listening for the thunder of motorcycles, moved on downtown. Only the wail of sirens pursued him. Canal Street was almost deserted: white men stood out in front of the bars beside the Jung Hotel, drinks in hand, scrutinizing the inhabitants of passing cars; teenagers in seamen's fatigues and T-shirts — the uniform of the Channel — moved furtively along the darkened storefronts. Comiski didn't see a single black face on the street or in the cars that jumped the traffic signals and careened through the Quarter. A ragged convertible kept abreast of him for a half a block before pulling slowly away, the muscular white arm dangling from one window trailing a machete along the curb. From the direction of Beauregard Park came the rattle of small arms fire.

He walked down Burgundy, ducked into Cosimo's. Three men wearing bowling shirts emblazoned with the emblem of the Sewerage and Water Board were hunched over the bar, drinking rum and Coke; a skinny gap-toothed barmaid in a red crepe halter sat opposite them, hugging her bare arms. They stared at Comiski.

He ordered a double shot of bourbon, tried to catch his breath. Yes, he thought, they tried to kill you: it was no night to be out and about. No, indeed. People were doing untoward things to one another. The girl slowly poured his drink; she kept glancing at the door.

One of the bowlers said, "Seen any niggers out there?"

"Not a one."

Comiski threw down the whiskey; his stomach yawned. The barmaid reluctantly poured another.

The man snorted. "Don't suppose that means there ain't none."

"Suppose not," Comiski said.

151

"There's plenty niggers round here. You just cain't see 'em tonight."

"You've got a point — there could be a whole raft of unseen niggers out there, and we'd never know it."

The man swiveled around on the stool, rested thick freckled hands on his knees.

"Well, now," he said. "Why don't you go grab us a couple?"

"Not me, brother. I'm here to tell you there's nothing trickier than grabbing hold of an unseen nigger. Especially at night. I know because that was my job in the war — catching unseen niggers."

"That so?"

"It is. We used to dig a big hole in the middle of the path leading through the mangoes, cover it over with branches and bright shiny objects. I'm telling you, some nights it used to rain unseen niggers."

The man slipped off the stool.

"Crawford," the barmaid warned.

"And what did you do with them niggers, after you catched 'em?" Crawford asked.

"That was the tough part — trying to figure out which were the unseen niggers and which were the average everyday ones." He finished his drink, added, "An unseen nigger isn't always what he seems."

That should do it, Comiski thought. He waited for the others to dismount: it was a paltry gesture, voluntarily dying at the hands of the Sewerage and Water Board. Crawford said, "Which war was that?"

"The Ubangi Stomp. Never been one to equal it."

The barmaid came around and opened the door. "Out!"

she said.

He got up to leave; Crawford told him, "Ordinarily I'd stomp your ass."

Comiski went out. Ordinarily, he thought, I wouldn't invite you. The filament in the broken streetlight flashed and sputtered, flooding the clapboard facades of the houses with alternating light and shadow; he touched the telephone poles as he walked, like a blind man. He hadn't eaten: his stomach inhaled the bourbon. A patrol car screamed across the intersection behind him. Comiski thought it was bearing down on him, stumbled on a front stoop, and fell heavily against the screen door. No one came to investigate; there wasn't a light in a single window on the block.

He sat on the steps, wanting to do something — to act: there seemed to be no rational alternative to immobility. Tea the intransigent, the poor murderous bastard! Comiski saw him sprawled on the tray beneath Gomer's knife, riddled with shotgun pellets like a slab of acoustical tile. Had Carrie gone down in the same barrage of fire, or was she heaped in the middle of the mall, swept by clouds of tear gas? Would Gomer get that smooth skin beneath his antiseptic hands?

He looked up toward Rampart, saw the dark silhouette of Parks's old apartment house leaning against the adjacent building, remembered the three abandoned white people crouched among their furniture, waiting for someone to pay their rent. Now there was a cause: Comiski could provide money, have them moved back into the building with their thirteen cats; he could dispense change for soft drinks. *What we need is an unaffected party.* Here I am, he thought. The most unaffected of parties.

153

The house was dark and forbidding. Comiski approached it cautiously, paused outside the periphery of upthrust chair legs: hiding there was an unshaven syphilitic, his demented sister, and outraged mother, and they *needed* Comiski. He called softly, heard the voice of a man on the edge of suicidal drunkenness. Go, he reasoned. Go find a drink and a bar rail and call a Yellow.

Instead, he rapped on top of the old refrigerator; there was no response other than the distant lament of sirens. Comiski picked his way among the furniture, upset a row of bottles; the sound of breaking glass was oppressive. He struck a match. The ground was littered with candy wrappers and empty metal snuffboxes, but the people were gone; Comiski felt cheated, as if someone had taken them away just to prevent him from doing good works. He began to search for his beneficiaries, knocked over a lamp that collided noisily with the drainpipe, kicked aside cheap aluminum chairs; his stomach was pressed against the iron bedstead, and with unexpected malice he flung it out onto the pavement.

Go, he thought. Go now.

Comiski went back to the refrigerator, jerked open the door. The stench of rotting flesh was so powerful that he was propelled backward against the wooden column supporting the eaves; he clamped a hand over his mouth and nose. Only something large and thoroughly mortified could smell that bad. He fumbled with a match, but it broke; the second one blazed, illuminating a mass of damp fur and a dozen blank tumescent eyes — the refrigerator was full of dead cats.

He slammed the door, stood in the midst of the scattered furniture, and tried not to vomit. A squad car turned the corner, listing heavily to one side, the tires screaming in protest: it was too late to act, too late to run.

The car pulled up in front of the house; two cops got out, swung the beams of their flashlights from the iron bedstead to Comiski's face, blinding him.

"What happened to these people?" he demanded.

The men approached him warily; from behind the two intercepting orbs of light came the sound of a familiar voice.

"My, my. Big Comiski."

It was Novak. One of the flashlights was extinguished; Comiski was shoved up against the column, where deft hands frisked him.

"Where's your animal act?" Comiski asked.

"I'm handling this interview, Mister Reporter, not you. How come you're out on a night like this, tearing up people's property?"

"You sent them to Mandeville. You and the judge."

"Shut up," Novak said. "You won't be asking any questions from now on — you and your kind are on the outside."

"You goddamn hoodlum..."

Novak's bulky uniformed figure obstructed the light. Comiski heard a quick intake of breath, felt a hard blunt object drive into his solar plexus, collapsing his lungs: it was unexpected and painful, and he threw up all over his assailant's feet.

"Why you goddamn drunk media bastard..."

Comiski anticipated another blow, raised his arm. He had the sensation that his windpipe was clogged; points of yellow and purple light swarmed before his eyes. The handcuff grasped his wrist, wrenched him off balance. He fell to his

155

knees, struggled in the dirt until he felt the other cuff: he was chained to the post.

Novak's partner said, "Looks like a case of resisting arrest to me. A mighty bad case of resisting."

"The smart-asses are on the downgrade," Novak said. "From now on things are gonna be some different."

Comiski stood, slid the chain up the smooth wooden column. He watched as Novak's partner placed his flashlight on the ground; both policemen took off their uniform jackets and folded them neatly over the back of a chair. Novak rolled up his shirt sleeves.

"High time," he said, "for law and order. We're cracking down on the kooks, queers, kinks, and Commies — the deadwood and the deadwood sympathizers."

Comiski couldn't swallow: he had the impression he had been in that position before, would have said or done anything to prevent what was about to happen.

"And I'm gonna start," Novak said, "by cleaning my shoes."

CARRIE hugged the bundle, lifted the suitcase, and ran. A pair of headlights stabbed through a hole in the ruined wall — rotating spots illuminating a stage cluttered with angular pipe fixtures and heaped rubble — groping for the fugitive. Right on cue, she thought, stumbling among ragged nail-infested boards and driving bits of mortar into her bare knees. She bent forward until the headlights had swept over her, heard the car accelerate and the crunch of heavy metal dragging tarmac as it took the intersection at a bound. Outsiders — they didn't know the ruts.

She held her position, waited for the enemy to circle. It

was always like that: she seemed to make her move at just the wrong moment. No sense of timing, no stage presence. The chorus of sirens sang to her; it was the oldest tune she knew. The car didn't return, and she stood and touched her leg, the warm slick of blood, dragged the suitcase toward the cafe.

The windows were dark, tattered shades drawn; the swaybacked building sat on its concrete blocks like a derelict ark, waiting for a flood. It might have been deserted, promised no sanctuary. Carrie needed someone to blame, and she cursed Tea between breaths for leaving her alone, uninformed: she even had their things — old clothes, cigarettes, five hundred grams of raw heroin. Enough to buy this burg, Tea said, and yet he stuffed it into a coffee can and hid it in a rat hole, seemed to forget. What was that man after?

She scrambled up the cafe steps, pounded on the door. The shade stirred and settled; Carrie rattled the knob, kicked against the baseboard.

"Clarence!" she called. "Hey, man, open this door!"

She heard the elaborate system of bolts and locks being unraveled. The door swung back into semi-darkness; Clarence stood stolidly beside it, naked except for a sleeveless undershirt that reached no farther than his navel and a pair of red socks held up by garters. His hair stood out like a mass of magnetized iron filings.

"What you want?" he whispered.

"Where's the Prince?"

"Cain' say."

"Jupe, the others — they here?"

Clarence slowly shook his head, rolled vast comatose eyes.

"Gone," he said. "All gone."

"I'll just have a look."

He barred her way. "No, suh. You de Prince's woman. De Prince done made a whole mess'a trouble fo' us colored folks. Don' want no trouble like dat. No, suh. You git along now."

"Let me in," Carrie pleaded.

"Git along, lil' fox."

She pushed futilely against his stumpy body; he closed the door, mashing her fingers against the jamb.

"Why you nigger!..." she called.

The security system was reassembled; Clarence shuffled off toward the back of his cafe, mumbling to himself.

Carrie sucked her knuckles, tried to think. She had to lie in someplace, to cover herself and their stash: it was no night to be dragging the main. The sirens sang on, forever shifting, heedless of time and direction; they drew her toward sleep. Cautiously she descended the steps, her body registering its resistance to any more traveling. Her lips seemed strung together on viscous strands of saliva; her eyes were socketed in dry feverish flesh, dazzled by the streetlamp's feeble glow.

The sound of motorcycles carried up from Poydras. She could see headlights eddying beneath the traffic signal, the beams jostled by the street's broken surface — three crazy eyes weaving into focus — heard the hysterical whine of gears as the machines opened up. Carrie stood hugging the bundle in dumb fright, watched them approach with fascination and an odd sense of moral justification: they were on to her, and it was all Tea's fault.

She crouched, ran across the brittle stumps of burned weeds. Something dark and menacing emerged from beneath the cafe, lunged at her; she saw the chain lengthen and grow taut as a dog with matted fur hanging from its belly heaved up onto its hind legs, blunt teeth and gums exposed, and collapsed in a spasm of drowned ferocity. She heard only the din of motorcycles. The dog was up and after her, throwing itself against the chain's limitation; Carrie crawled under the cafe, abandoned the suitcase, dragged the shopping bag after her. She was pursued among the discarded newspapers and Dr. Pepper bottles, came to rest against a concrete support. The dog wallowed closer, lunged against the chain until she thought he would bring the building down.

The motorcycles performed a sort of quadrille in the street, the headlights blazing among the forest of pilings. Carrie expected the dog to bark, to turn toward the new intruders, but it continued to silently stalk her, hampered by the chain. A dull explosion rained glass across the porch; bare feet thundered overhead, and someone fell in the room directly above her. The veil of grime drifting across the headlights' glare settled on her hands like black snow. Carrie pressed one cheek against the cool stone and waited.

The motorcycles made another pass, fell into formation three abreast and lunged up the street, leaving darkness and a wail of sorrow as Clarence prayed for deliverance. The floorboards dipped and protested as he lumbered about the room on his knees, his voice on top of her.

"Lawd, Lawd, Lawd God a'mighty how... how come you done let dem chirren... chirren o' de devil come bustin'... bustin' in, Lawd ain't You got... got no 'preciation?"

Carrie rocked herself to the rhythm of his lament. She had done her bit — Oh, yes, Lord, she had done that, all right. *Ain't you got no 'preciation?* She tried to visualize the face of the

Lord, saw the eyes of Doctor Porteus bright and damp behind his bifocals, his lame smile: he was telling her something important, and she couldn't understand a word.

"Shit, girl," she whispered. "Your baby belongs to welfare."

The dog growled in response, tugged at the chain; she stared at the dark silhouette, slipped toward panic. You're nowhere. She gagged, but the tears wouldn't come, touched her breasts, ran one hand over the flat of her stomach: she was dry, needed a boost. Inside the bundle was the kit and enough stuff to keep her stoned for a century; it was a terrifying thought.

Carrie opened the shopping bag, felt for the coffee can. She arranged the syringe, spoon, and matches on the square of dirty towel, slipped off one sandal and tossed it out among the weeds; the dog bounded after it, began to maul the bit of leather and plastic, and she crept forward and pulled his battered water pan beyond the chain's reach. Carrie opened the can, kindled a fire with strips of newsprint, spooned dark water from the pan. The dog returned to watch, rested its head on its paws.

The needle glinted yellow, emerged from the flame a burnished black. So easy, she thought: you're graduating.

Overhead, Clarence continued to admonish his god.

COMISKI woke up inside a cage. He was in motion, gliding along behind the siren's dirge that cut cleanly through the night. A rotating blue light swept the fronts of buildings, the hoods of cars, stark faces, bathed them in electric hues of madness; through the mesh he could see the outlines of two uniformed men, the dancing embers of their cigarettes. Static flowed from the radio, interspersed with the voices of men

involved in a struggle at the end of some long corridor. The
pain deep inside his kidney was alive — a writhing serpent
agitated by the rocking motion of the squad car; Comiski's
trousers were wet.

The car dipped, sped through the familiar archway and into
the basement parking lot of the police station. The concrete
chamber was full of the plaint of dying sirens and sweeping
lights; he was hustled out of the car and across to the elevator.
Comiski discovered that he limped, that the chain on the
handcuffs rattled with each step. He was dirty and befouled and
he didn't care: the world had wobbled, shifting the battle lines
— he decided he was on the wrong side. When the elevator
doors parted and he found himself confronted by a dozen men
— most of whom he recognized — Comiski thought he should
acknowledge them. I know you men are wondering why I have
gathered you together...

They hurried past without seeing him; Novak and his
partner shoved him into the metal box, and they ascended in
silence.

Comiski was greeted by the green walls of the Identification
Bureau, the smells of musty clothes, cigar smoke, and spilled
Pepsi. The frame prototypes of fingerprints surrounded
him like the bloodshot eyes of outraged relatives; a nebbish
detective wearing elastic armbands and a green plastic visor
grinned at him.

"Comiski! What you done now, boy?"

Novak prodded him toward the desk. "I want you on
record," he whispered.

"You're not gonna charge him?" the detective said; he held
up hands black with ink. "We're busy enough."

161

"I got charges, all right. Disturbing and resisting."

"I want to see you in front of a judge," Comiski said.

The detective looked Comiski over with genuine pity. He squeezed a coil of ink from the tube, rolled it flat, gently took his hand and pressed the index finger against the sticky surface of the glass; as his finger was being rolled over the white matting of the card, Comiski moved his hand and smudged the print.

"Just keep it up," Novak whispered. "You'll never see a judge."

The detective patiently replaced the card, finished the job; Comiski was led away. Negroes with manacles on their ankles waited in line at the lockup, patrolled by sheriff's deputies who prodded the faltering into standing position. The walls were brushed with blood. Comiski was given precedence over the black men; a balding cop with stained dentures and suspenders printed with dueling pistols winked at him, directed him to the canvas backdrop, and held a board across his chest. The sun burst. Comiski was turned to one side, and this time the camera drilled him through the temple.

The guard swung open the lockup. Novak gave him a final push; Comiski turned to spit, but the door swung shut. He followed a warder in a green uniform along the low passageway filled with a single strident echo. Black men were pressed together in the cells; more men lay in the passage with their ankles chained to the bars. The warder shook his head in disgust, kicked them aside; Comiski stepped precariously among the rubble of bodies. The concrete ducts edging the cells ran with urine and some unidentifiable flotsam.

He said to the warder, "Not here."

"There's nowhere else."

The bars slammed shut. Dark faces swam before him; heat seemed to rain down from some device on the ceiling, shattered against white tiles. Comiski looked at the drain in the middle of the cell floor: the barbed mouth of a suffocating fish. He stepped over it, toiled up the incline, slipped and fell. Each time he tried to stand he skidded on the slimy tiles and went down again; his hands were covered with someone else's blood. He began to crawl, avoiding a Negro who touched his mordant lips with tentative fingers; he had teeth marks in one ear, and a thin blue laceration ran down into the collar of his shirt. A sonorous voice choked with spittle sang, "*I'm wa-alkin' the floor over you...*"

He hit his head against a wooden bench, grabbed it and held on. The echo faltered, changed to keening; a guard thrust a fire hose between the bars, directed the bronze nozzle toward the drain, and bodies scrambled over each other in an effort to get clear. The din of lamentation arched higher; another guard ran along the passage, clubbing the bars. A shaft of water struck the floor with force, and the cell filled with a bright red mist.

Comiski stood up on the bench, began to scream.

PART 3:

Easy Out

E ARLY MORNING sunlight warmed the bas-relief above the steps of the Criminal Courts building, seemed to wash the stone's surface, revealing decades of filth collected in crevices outlining the figures of men and women arrested in a cold rural landscape. Carrie stared up at the lifeless forms supported by fluted columns — limbs without joints, eyes without pupils — tried to understand; a Latin inscription in letters three feet tall, dusted with soot, told her nothing. She felt menaced by the sweep of the granite sickle, fast against unyielding grain. If that was the scene in ancient times, she was glad she had missed it.

The foyer of the building was deserted. The elevators were locked shut; the vast room, with its marble staircase and domed convoluted ceiling, seemed dedicated solely to the containment of the stale odor of cigar smoke. Lord, Carrie thought, what a place! The thought itself seemed to echo, returned to her as the rustling of her shopping bag and the padding of her bare feet across the cool stone floor. The hallways stretching in both directions were lined with paneled doors; sunlight filtered through towering unwashed windows touched the deserted corridors with warmth.

She saw an old man sitting behind a vinyl-topped counter in one corner of the foyer. Beside him stood a stainless steel coffee machine, draped in a towel; he rested his head against the padlocked cabinet bearing a decal advertising Dr. Pepper. He seemed to be asleep. Carrie walked up to the counter, saw that the man held a pint of apricot flavored vodka in one hand and an empty paper cup in the other.

"Who's that?" he said, without opening his eyes.

Carrie didn't answer, stared at his moist trembling lids.

"It's Thanksgiving," the man said. "You expect me to stay open on Thanksgiving?"

"I reckon not." She thought she smelled food: chocolate, cheap pastries, salted nuts. "Whereabouts is the morgue?"

He gestured with his pint bottle. "End of the hall. On the left."

Carrie hesitated. "There's nothing in your cup," she said.

"It's early, girl. Give me time."

She moved off, followed the sound of static. A single door was open onto the hallway; the board above was stenciled with peeling gold leaf letters that read PRESS, and inside she could see dingy green walls and a view of barred windows. If Comiski was there, he could help her: it was a break she hadn't counted on.

Carrie stopped inside the doorway. A young man sat punching at the keyboard of a teletype machine; the sleeves of his shirt were neatly rolled, and he wore a striped tie that reminded her of Christmas. Peanut brittle wrapped in white tissue paper and cheap ribbon, peppermint candy canes that melted in the December heat and stuck to her fingers: she could taste the gritty sugar. Carrie tried to see Comiski in this nice clean college boy, felt that she was losing ground, would never catch up with what was really happening.

"I read in the paper where they killed him," she said. "Is that right?"

"Probably." The young man smiled. "Who is it you're looking for?"

"I'm looking for Tea. They killed him, then?"

"You mean Teague the anarchist?" He stood up, almost overturning his chair. "Don't tell me you knew Teague?"

"You could say I knew him."

"Well, now." The young man wet his lips. "This is a break. Who did you say you were?"

"I didn't say. It doesn't matter. Tell me if he's dead."

"Yes. Very dead, I'm afraid."

The telephone on his desk began to ring. Carrie could see bare tree limbs outside the window, the uniform trajectories of a pair of pigeons framed against the sky. She felt almost relieved: her work was cut out.

"Hot damn," the young man said. "If you'll just take a chair, I want to talk to you. Now don't go 'way."

Carrie waited until he reached for the telephone, then went quickly down the hall. *Yes, very dead...* She sensed it, woke up that morning to a dawn the color of gun metal and the smell of burning and knew it had finally happened. There was something deadly in all that silence: the touch of the wind, low curdled clouds swept away like so much trash. When the sun finally rose, it offered no comfort, seemed to

167

define rather than eliminate darkness; she found herself keeping to the shadows. On the corner of Tulane and Loyola she had stopped before an automatic newspaper dispenser and read the headlines through the scuffed plastic cover. She knew none of the particulars because the paper was folded over, and she had no change.

Carrie opened a door marked **ORLEANS PARISH CORONER**. The stairway smelled of chemicals; she descended, passed a desk piled with records bound in foolscap, sprinkled with cigarette ashes and bits of crumpled note paper — there was no one to receive her. The smell grew stronger. At the foot of the stairs she saw two swinging doors; one of them was propped open by an empty stretcher, and she couldn't look at the drab green blanket caked with blood.

The morgue was filled with light that reflected in the white tiles, glinted from the polished handles of metal vaults. An old Negro woman lay naked on a stainless steel tray, reposed and oddly sexless; a white man in an apron watched Carrie from his perch beside the body.

"What you want?" he whispered.

"I want the remains."

The man climbed down from his stool, the knife rattling against the metal as he slid it down toward the woman's feet. She saw that one lens of his glasses was covered with a black patch: there was something about the place that seemed to affect peoples' eyes.

"Whose remains is that?" the man asked.

"Tea's. I'm the next of kin."

"You mean Teague?"

Carrie could barely hear him. She felt her annoyance

growing: it wasn't a big thing to ask.

"You talk to Homicide, girl?"

"I got no truck with Homicide," she said. "You just give me the body."

"Wouldn't call it a body." The man grinned. "Ain't much left."

Carrie dug her fingernails into her palm: they were quicker than she figured.

"All right, mister. Ashes, then."

"Ashes, shit." He picked up the telephone and began to dial. "You want a member, some of the boys got fingers in alcohol..."

She moaned, clawed at the amorphous face. The glasses fell and shattered against the tiles; the little man groped along the edge of the desk, screaming.

"*Leroy! Leroy, git this nigger...*"

A uniformed figure with foreshortened arms lunged into the light, frightened and confused. Carrie picked up her shopping bag and fled through the swinging doors; climbing the stairs, she felt herself pursued by a hideous choking sound that came from her own lips. She stumbled out into the hallway, where the young man from the press room stood with outstretched arms. There was a pencil behind his ear; he gripped a sheaf of blank paper.

"Here you are," he said brightly. "Now if you'll just tell me exactly how it was..."

"No!" she shrieked, pushing past him. She ran toward the foyer; he called after her, his voice echoing along the corridor, but she didn't look back.

THE ALLEYWAY was deserted. A blue sky menaced the strip of open space between the prison and the courts building — a glass lid descending upon a coffin, trapping the motionless humid air and the smells of frying grits and coffee strong as creosote. Contesting black men's voices tumbled with the clouds of steam from the open kitchen window, punctuated by the clatter of metal cauldrons. Trash cans brimming with potato peelings lined one wall; beyond them was parked a department transport truck, and underneath the canvas cover truncheons were stacked as neatly as firewood amid the jumble of blue helmets and khaki uniforms. The absence of the wail of sirens was strange, unworldly.

Comiski pressed the brown paper envelope against his chest and followed the turnkey to the front gate. The old man's trousers swirled about his thin legs; his gait was matched by that of his pet — an arthritic bulldog with an inflamed rectum and suppurating eyes that had been the mascot of the sheriff's deputies for years. Dog and master tottered toward the end of the alley, paused and turned at the same moment, regarded Comiski with disbelief.

The old man said, "How come you got yourself into such a mess?"

He couldn't answer. The dog shifted expectantly; the turnkey shook his head, peered through the grill, opened the low door in the gate.

"You watch yourself," he said, helping Comiski over the threshold.

A line of black faces extended out to the street and down the pavement for almost a block: women waiting for a glimpse of the inside and a missing husband or relative or boyfriend.

Comiski's heart quickened. Maybe, just maybe. He eased along the line, looking at each suppliant, encountered only unfamiliar and hostile eyes averted in disgust; a woman in cerise stretch pants said, "Git on, trash!" and raised her umbrella threateningly. Carrie wasn't there — no one was waiting in line for Comiski.

He reached the corner, leaned against the stanchion supporting the bus stop sign. The island in the center of Broad was littered with paper; the breeze blowing up from Lake Pontchartrain smelled predominantly of burning rubber. Except for an occasional heavy truck barreling across town, there was no traffic. Comiski waited; the pain in his kidney ebbed and flowed — a continuous scald — but the organ might have been housed in someone else's flesh: he remained aloof. When a bus pulled over the horizon, he grappled with the brown paper envelope in an attempt to get his wallet out. His fingers were encrusted with dried blood: it was as if he wore mittens, and he tore the paper in his haste, spilling wallet, keys, and watch about his feet.

The bus didn't stop. The driver and another man in uniform stared at Comiski and rolled past; he retrieved his valuables and began the long walk down Tulane. In spite of the limp and the kidney, his body functioned, carried itself along with a curious listless momentum. The earth trembled as the trucks roared past; clouds of exhaust swarmed about the rising sun — the air seemed full of portent, stirred by the rush of wings. He was trembling, his progress unimpeded: Comiski was simply cold, unaffected by the degrading phenomenon of delirium tremens. His toes and fingers froze, lengthened as spines of ice. The features of his face felt distended by the cold; the hard shells of his lips emitted a sputtering sound.

Don't stop.

You were there, he told himself. Starkers. Madness arrives on ferocious wings: starkers and ravers.

His head filled with ringing — a sad persistent sound that grew steadily louder, then receded, mounted again. It was the burglar alarms in the liquor stores along the avenue, protesting violations of property long since completed. A helicopter passed somewhere overhead, loud but unseen, clattered away to the east.

Don't stop now.

Canal Street was deserted. Comiski did stop, huddled on a bench beneath the statue of Molly the Marine, hugged and rocked himself. Gradually the trembling subsided; he slept fitfully, kept waking to the vision of pavement and the threat of a bull dike in bronze crushing him underfoot. His mouth was full of the taste of corroded metal. He had an overwhelming desire to scratch his armpits, his crotch, and the bottoms of his feet; his breathing had a rasp to it.

Cars moved cautiously along the street. A trolley turned the corner of Carondelet, shuttled down toward the monolith of the Trade Mart; people began to gather on the pavement in front of Walgreen's — the only drugstore open on Thanksgiving — and Comiski hobbled off to join them. He watched his own reflection drift through the static garish world of display windows, vaulting without substance the reefs of new shoes and cameras and transistor radios. The man he saw was one of hundreds in soiled clothes who slept in LaFayette Square, scrounged handouts at the back door of Mother's, and occasionally endured a sermon for a free bunk and a meal at the Ozanam Inn.

Comiski went into Walgreen's, where he bought a newspaper and a quart of Jim Beam; then he caught the trolley up St. Charles.

The paper described the fighting as a "civil disturbance." The police reported two deaths: a demented old woman who was crushed beneath the riot truck — "emergency communications and coordination van" — and a known narcotics peddler, Tobias Teague — alias Prince Tea, Teetotaler, and plain Tea. The article said Tea's body was burned almost beyond recognition; there was no mention of his revolutionary band, nothing about Carrie. The department was playing down its disorders. Comiski could imagine the rigged inquest attended by dozing piebald flunkies from City Hall: he was still afraid, smelled it in his own sweat and the detritus of prison that clung to his clothes. He pictured Gomer's lily-white hands setting aside the surgical knife and delving into the open wound of his own stomach, palms outward. He dreaded that indignation, more now than ever. If he was dying of internal injuries, even the bourbon wouldn't preserve him; he could only hide his carcass away, postpone the moment of discovery and investigation. Comiski the stinker.

He rode past LaFayette Square, climbed down in front of the Eureka Hotel: it was one place they wouldn't check.

The desk clerk wore an army shirt with one sleeve hanging empty; his fingers were stained with nicotine, and he drummed them on the counter, regarded Comiski skeptically.

"I want a room with a bathtub," Comiski told him. "And a view."

"All our rooms got views. Let's see three bills fifty."

173

He took a five-dollar bill from his wallet. "And ice," he added.

The man grunted, handed him a key attached to a block of wood; Comiski slowly climbed the stairs. The room contained two single beds separated by a lacquered radio that served as a nightstand, and above it hung a lithograph in bright pastels of Christ, bleeding heart exposed, eyes cast toward heaven in what might have been exasperation. Comiski raised the window, pushed open the shutters, took in his view of dingy brick and wrought-iron balconies across St. Charles. The bourbon felt heavy in his hand: capable of miracles — the stuff of dreams.

He set the bottle on the radio, went into the bathroom, and turned on the water in the tub. Easy, he thought, you're almost there. Steam rose from the spigot; he realized that the bells had stopped ringing.

Comiski listened to the knocking — the death rattle. He opened the door and saw the desk clerk standing in the dark hallway, holding a chipped bowl full of ice cubes; the man strained to see past him into the room.

"You want some pussy?"

"Not today," Comiski said. "In a couple of hours bring food — something hot."

"Cafeteria don't open till noon. We got hot tamales."

"All right, tamales."

He handed the man another bill, took the bowl of ice, and shut the door: time to begin. He picked up the bourbon bottle and went back into the bathroom, undressed, and stood over the toilet, fists on naked hips. The pain in his kidneys waned, but the sight of bright red urine brought on the trembling again and the sputtering sound over which he had no control. Comiski sat on the edge of the tub and tried to mix a drink, sloshed whiskey and ice water into the glass and drank off half the mixture. In the street below he saw a tourist bus lumber past, filled with middle-aged couples wearing earphones and leaning forward in their seats, trying to spot a degenerate. Life goes on.

Glass and bottle in hand, Comiski crept into the tub. A woman in a green slip stepped out on the balcony opposite to water her blighted chrysanthemums; she saw Comiski and scowled, ducked back inside.

"Hail to thee," he said, raising his glass. "Heartfelt felicitations."

He felt his brain expanding like warm dough in a plastic bag. There were things to be thankful for: Novak's charges were simply dropped, he was alive. A trolley ground past on its pitted rails, rattling the balconies; from a bar on the corner came the lamentations of Johnny Cash, though the words of the song were indistinguishable. Comiski settled deeper into the water. It was hours before he had to move.

DELAVERNE lowered his head in silent prayer. The aromas of roast turkey, oyster stuffing, baked sweet potatoes topped with a crust of melted marshmallows, raisins and shelled walnuts, hot buttermilk biscuits and pan-browned giblet gravy combined forces in assaulting his senses, subverting him from his purpose; Delaverne found himself salivating over the concept of divine intervention. From the living room came the muffled sound of the television set, the sportscaster's voice rising to the level of urgency calculated to excite. Delaverne strained to

175

hear: something about an end run. The crowd roared on cue, lapsed into the silence of ignorance and uncertainty, waiting for a sign from the referee — the supreme arbiter.

"Amen," said Delaverne and his wife in unison.

Unenlightened about the outcome of the play, he began to carve the turkey. Soft white meat folded back from the blade, heightened his anticipation: his wife knew a pot from a skillet, no doubt about it.

Delaverne pointed the knife at a bottle standing between the sliced tomatoes and the apple pie. "What's that?" he asked.

"Wine." His wife smiled. "Sauteme. I put it in the icebox. I thought for Thanksgiving..."

"Beer'll do me. Today and every day."

He poured his can of Jax into an enameled mug bearing the crest of the Fraternal Order of Police. The sight of the crescent moon filled him with disdain: it was no more than a social club — a dead eclipsed planet compared with the force with which he had become acquainted. A new sun had risen.

Delaverne and his wife hunched over their meal, fed in silence; finally she said, "I don't know what's become of Joy. I always thought Thanksgiving was for the family."

"Your sister still going out with that spic?"

"I suppose she is." His wife sighed. "Jesus isn't a bad boy, really."

"*Jesus!*" Delaverne mocked. "That's disgusting. If Joy's little greaseball backs his Mustang over my winter grass again, I'll..."

He paused: careless driving wasn't an excuse for cutting a man in half, even a Panamanian with a sacrilegious name and a suspicious lot of ready cash. Delaverne reminded himself to

check up on old Jesus — run his name through the grinder;
you never knew.

Breathing with difficulty, he devoured the asparagus in
aspic. Tiny beads of perspiration appeared on his upper lip;
he wiped them away. He had never considered the possibility
that an upper lip might sweat — it was a peculiar sensation,
and demeaning. Delaverne still touched the hairless expanse
gingerly, like an amputee caressing the stump. The mustache
had been with him for ten years; one minute beneath the razor,
and it ceased to exist. The absence of those wiry bristles made
him uneasy.

"It looks real nice," his wife said. "Makes you look so much
younger. I was saying to Joy..."

"It's not worth talking about."

Delaverne belched into his napkin, watched as his wife set
a slab of the pie before him, edged with strips of cheddar. He
roused himself, demolished the wedge, and then another.

"Real good," Delaverne conceded.

His wife averted her eyes, touched her close gray curls.

"I was out at the Home," she said, "the one Jesus told Joy
about. It's so nice — they were very encouraging."

"It's not something we ought to rush into."

"We're not rushing. Why, we've been talking about
adoption for years. Doctor Porteus says all we have to do now
is decide."

"No time to be raising children, what with the mess the
country's in today. I wouldn't feel right."

"Somebody's got to raise them — they're already here."
She began to fold and unfold her hands. "It'd be real nice, no
problems. You could have somebody to go hunting with —

you know, later on."

"I don't need somebody to go hunting with. What I need is..." Delaverne stood. "Listen here, how do you know who the father is? Might be bad blood — most likely is, or else they wouldn't be shoving the kids off on decent people."

"They got all kinds of records out at the Home — everything we need. There's no problems, Verne."

"But how can you be sure?" he said. "How can we ever be *really* sure?"

"Wouldn't have to matter all that much. I mean, if you raise a child right..."

Delaverne slammed his meaty palm down against the printed linen cloth.

"If you think for one minute that I'm going to feed the offspring of some goddamn do-nothing..."

"Please," she said.

"Please nothing. Sometimes you make me sick to my stomach."

His wife began to cry. Delaveme was short of breath; he placed a hand on her shoulder, felt her shake with the sobs.

"I've got so much on my mind," he said, and added, "All right, I'll think about it."

He went into the living room. The strap of his shoulder holster was held in the outstretched hand of a headless Greek deity in plaster of paris — an anniversary present from Joy — and he buckled himself into the apparatus with determination. Before stowing the Smith and Wesson he gave the cartridges a perfunctory check, his eyes wandering to the television set. Tiny figures raced mindlessly across the screen, upsetting one another; the dark background of the crowd writhed, rejoiced.

Delaverne would miss his games, but he didn't mind: the idea of working on Thanksgiving pleased him. His work was for the good of the country, was in keeping with tradition. He imagined healthy open-faced seventeenth-century men in curious hats sitting around a rough-hewn table, their shirt sleeves rolled up to reveal arms used to manual labor: they inclined their heads over the empty dishes, leaned together in a confidential sort of way — honest capable men dealing with the problems at hand, combating the forces of subversion lurking in a vast encompassing wilderness. Delaverne was proud of that heritage; he noted with satisfaction that the founding Pilgrim fathers had scorned all facial hair.

He opened the front door, paused to catch his breath. The night before he had been reluctant to step into the street and take up the battle; he recognized the weakness for moralizing when the situation demanded action, tempered his self-contempt. There was time yet.

Delaverne's wife stared at the mutilated apple pie; he decided not to disturb her.

GUSTS OF wind riding up from the Gulf of Mexico trailed scraps of cloud across a clear November sky. A single engine stunt plane banked and rolled directly above the racetrack — its angry drone barely discernible — and spelled out in fragile streams of white smoke the one word: DIXIE. Almost immediately the child's block letters grew ragged and illegible; the simple message disintegrated before the plane could escape beyond the eaves of the clubhouse, where dangling bits of red, yellow, and blue cloth danced like bright frenetic butterflies. Politicians, promoters, and their women sat

179

stolidly behind the clubroom's tinted glass and stared down at the oblong of turf and the betting board riddled with points of light as it transmitted the rush of ever-changing odds. The outdoor stands were crowded with men in open shirts and wives unpacking bags stuffed with sandwiches, potato chips, and pecan pie wrapped in wax paper; the skirt of a matron hawking beer billowed up to reveal rolls of stocking choking dimpled thighs, her stack of cups tumbling and scattering over the track, where prancing horses shied away. The smell of fresh broken earth warmed in the sun competed with those of straw and manure from the paddock, vanished before the wind.

Bettors eddied in the aisles and in the passageways leading to the stalls, anxious for it all to begin. The mellifluous, too-familiar voice of the mayor launched a final inanity over the public address system, died in echo. At last a squat figure dressed in hunting red and black mounted a block beside the finish line and blew through his silver post horn, heralding the opening race with what would be his only sober performance of the entire season; the crowd was already cheering.

Comiski leaned against the railing at the edge of the chute, sipped tepid beer from a paper cup. His new sunglasses — bought from Walgreen's on his way back across town — tinged the world with pink and minimized contrast: he was reminded of diluted blood, shivered beneath the touch of his sweaty shirt. He was aware of the taste of stale tamales. The injured kidney refused to let him forget, though the pain was dulled by bourbon to a localized annoyance like flatulence or constipation — persistent tugs from the subconscious. He had, he remembered, an appointment.

A pair of policemen strolled through his rose-colored

vision. They seemed more lethal in repose; their clubs swung out with every other step on leather thongs, snapped back into their palms with a resounding *swack* that seemed to menace his own flesh. By now his fingerprints had been fed into the computerized mill of criminal detection, linking him with the straight razor; he went unrecognized.

Comiski waited until the cops were entering the clubhouse, then limped up the concrete steps and found a vacant seat. He always put something down on the first race of the season: it was a gesture of confidence — an affirmation of the system and appeasement of the gods. But this time he didn't bet. He sucked on the beer, watched as the bell sounded and the horses were away; screaming human beings stood and secluded him, and he was grateful.

Comiski sat out the first two races. A man in a madras jacket turned and stared at him; cop or tipster, he couldn't be sure, and he waited until the earnings were spread across the board before sidling out with the petty winners and taking up his position at the rail. Fresh jockeys urged their mounts out of the paddock and up onto the track. Their silk blouses rippled in the breeze, and for a moment Comiski forgot why he was there. It was his favorite slot: watching the horses go into the warm-up, trying to spot the gimps and the late-drinkers, the jockeys with haunted eyes. The losers. Comiski rarely picked a winner, but he could usually finger the loser; the spotted gray mare and her outsized rider trailing onto the track were not a duet upon which he would have stacked his pay check. He recognized Hoppy's freckled wrists protruding from the sleeves of a candy-apple green shirt that had once belonged to Littlebit. Hoppy hadn't bothered to shave; he slumped in the saddle, the cap tilted to shade a bruise at the edge of his right eye. Comiski congratulated himself: a veritable score.

Hoppy gazed down at Comiski. A cigarette stub rested behind one ear; his face registered nothing at all as he coaxed the sluggish horse into the routine with some semblance of professionalism. Driven Snow — a real loser. Comiski watched the odds lengthen on the board: someone else had noticed that cigarette.

Comiski made his way back toward the clubhouse. A dozen black people were huddled together in the track-level stands, heckled by bands of roving teen-agers and day trippers up from Houma and Biloxi to catch the races and to take part in the civil disturbances; the paired policemen kept the volunteers at bay. He reached the passageway leading to the betting stalls just as the bell sounded, but he didn't look back.

CARRIE pressed her body and the palms of her hands against the fender of a maroon Imperial, looked across the plain of parked cars toward the stables. The guard at the gate was armed; he checked an outward-bound car bearing Kentucky plates with perplexed belligerence — a paunchy old man who used to let her through without a pass, after grasping her wrist and whispering randy jokes in her ear until she consented to laugh. The toffee-colored handle of the revolver was pressed against his stomach like a distended member, grotesque and laughable; a piece of string ran from the trigger guard to the button on his trousers. Naturally he would be looking to kill her. Carrie was the owner of a horse — a bona fide contender — and she had business in her own stall, if all the racket hadn't scared away Tea's connection. It was the last thing she could do, before bowing out. *Ain't much left...*

She stepped out from between the cars. Two men appeared simultaneously at the edge of the lot, beside an empty horse trailer: Carrie loathed the sight of leather and silver bangles, felt her lip curl back, her hand tighten on the handle of her shopping bag as Bud and Grunt started toward her, looking awkward and childish away from their machines, their boots stirring up a cloud of dust. The runts. A sustained tumult carried across from the stands. The crowd was on to her, waiting eagerly for the contact — the crush; she felt the sharp unyielding gravel beneath her feet, smelled the odor of some autumn blossom lifted on the wind, watched Grunt slip one hand inside his jacket.

Carrie turned and ran. The shopping bag hindered her, banged against her thighs, snagged once on the handle of a car door; her feet made no sound, but her breathing was harsh and dry. The clubhouse beckoned like a papier-mâché citadel floating at the plain's edge. She thought she detected the drone of an airplane: up up and away. It wouldn't be long now.

She sprinted across the drive. A car skidded in the gravel; the blare of a horn upbraided her, but she kept moving, welcomed the smooth surface of concrete as she entered the passage leading to the ticket stalls. She dug into the pocket of her sweater and pushed a handful of coins through the half moon cut in plate glass, looked behind her. The two men came on, walking with a fast outlandish shuffle like desperadoes in an old western, hampered by their gear; Carrie wanted to laugh.

"Runts!" she told the ticket collector.

The man opened his mouth and revealed the dark cud of

chewing tobacco; he stared incredulously at her hair and her bare feet, started to protest, but Carrie brushed past.

DELAVERNE leaned forward and gripped the shoulders of his men. The attack of heartburn contracted his throat, brought warm saliva to his mouth; he held his breath until he saw the two leather jackets push through the turnstile.

The horn might have ruined everything: the stakeout, the tails — worse, his patient methodical preparation. It was too close; Bud had actually touched their car in passing, too rushed to bother with the passengers. Thanksgiving — Delaveme's lucky day.

"They'll git clear," one of the detectives complained.

The other man said, "How come they're chasing that nigger, that's what I'd like to know."

Delaverne silently commended himself: he recognized the girl — the mass of kinky hair, the high light skin tone — as Parks's woman. A dealer's octoroon. He was shrewd almost to a fault, keeping tabs on that black man's horse when the others forgot — the distinction between an administrator and an ordinary footsore patrolman. It promised to be a neat piece of work.

"All right," he said, "now easy does it."

The detectives stepped out of the car, scowling and rolling their shoulders, moved off down the passage. Delaverne climbed into the driver's seat and maneuvered the unmarked Ford into a vacant slot reserved for a track official; he had only to wait. He pressed one hand over his heart, as if to suppress the effect of acidity. Any sort of pain made him giddy, uneasy. There was always the possibility of extreme physical exertion, even of violence; he was on the job, however, and that made all the difference.

The anchor man jogged across the lot, scattering gravel, his face contorted with the effort; he leaned against the roof of the car to catch his breath.

"Found the cycles," he gasped, "behind the billboard yonder. Popped the tires."

"Why'd you do that?"

"Logical, Verne."

Delaverne didn't want his men acting on impulse. He could tell from the ring of grime around the detective's collar that he hadn't put on a fresh shirt that day; his feeling of uneasiness returned. He knew that his men lacked respect, thought many of Delaverne's decisions were uninspired and overcautious, his habits womanish. Some of the Citizens had implied that he didn't have the qualities required of members. Delaverne's anger resulted more from loneliness than insult: he would show them all.

"You check the stable?" he asked.

"Nothing in that direction, Verne."

"Well, keep at it."

The detective didn't attempt to disguise his resentment. Delaverne felt the rush of compassion that comes with righteousness: he could afford to humor this man.

"Could be trouble," he said. "Take along the scatter gun, if you want."

COMISKI wanted a drink. He remembered the quart of bourbon resting on the console radio in the hotel room, marveled at his restraint in not drinking it all, his capacity for self-deception: he had actually planned to get through the afternoon dry. Thanksgiving, time of plenty — lack of surfeit was unpatriotic. He couldn't be expected to gorge himself on fatty wieners and watery coleslaw, but whiskey was another matter. He eyed the bar from his position beneath the board; there was time to beat the rush. He could keep watch from the rail, elbows propped on either side of a glass.

He moved across the floor. A sigh went up from the crowd as new winnings were posted; bodies poured into the passageways, making for the stalls. Comiski allowed himself to be jostled — a modicum of pain — stared at the apparition ascending the stairs. Carrie crept along with one hand on the banister, gazing straight ahead; she crossed the floor without seeing him, bucking the tide of bettors. He recalled a naked girl all knees and elbows, skin that transmitted a strange subcutaneous radiance, eyes wide with meth: she had stripped away the flaccid underwear with disdain, casual and almost bored. *Oh, the smell of her...*

Comiski followed, kept the mass of hair in sight. People made way for that oddity; a man wearing a straw hat with tiny beer cans attached to the band turned and shouted, but Carrie pushed on. She entered the passage leading to the stands, took shelter on the leeward side of a woman in a baseball cap who was selling racing forms. Comiski's chest felt constricted; his kidney pulsed — the flashing bonus light in an overworked pinball machine. He almost turned away.

"I didn't figure you'd show," Carrie said.

"You're not going through with it? Not after what's happened."

She touched his arm. "This is all ritual."

"Listen, you better move. These good people don't seem to be taking to you."

Three men in green laborer's shirts formed an enclave beyond the display of racing forms, waiting for the trouble to begin; the jostling grew insistent.

"We're messing up the view," Comiski said.

Carrie placed a finger against her forehead.

"I wanted to tell you about that razor. Your prints weren't on it. You see, Andrew, you're back where you started. But if you still want to help, if you want to really *do* something..."

"Come on."

He took her arm, but she pulled away, delved into the shopping bag.

"I just give you the bundle," she said. "Tea had it all figured out."

"Like hell you do."

The woman gathered up her forms and moved away, muttering to Comiski; the men in green advanced. He stepped between them and the girl, felt his arms being pressed against his sides, waited for a blow that didn't come. Carrie began to stuff a package wrapped in newsprint into the pocket of his jacket.

"Goddammit!" he bellowed, wrenching himself free. One of the men stepped across and slapped at Carrie, but she ducked away.

"The stable," she whispered, her eyes bright and purposeful; she drifted backward with the crowd, toward the staircase.

Comiski swiveled, fists clenched, searching for his tormentors; the men in green dispersed, and the woman in the baseball cap made a brittle spitting sound. People stared at him. Comiski watched as Carrie reached the stairs and flung the shopping bag over the banister, then ran along the wall toward the far exit.

He understood. Bud emerged from the crowd, looked at Comiski and then went leaping down the steps.

He was frightened of the thing in his pocket, wanted to simply drop the bundle — an incriminating act. His hand recoiled from the touch of newspaper and string: Comiski the connection — the fool. It seemed that everyone in the hall was watching his self-conscious shuffle toward the men's lavatory. For several seconds he was pressed against the wall by the door of the rest room; his mind recorded particulars — fleshy faces, watery eyes, the reek of smoke and urine. He thought he saw Novak, then the nightmare masks in the prison drunk tank. Not again, never. He was getting out from under the brace of motorcycle boots and cops' vomit-splattered shoes, departing Tea's new citadel incubating beneath warm ashes, but first he was going to clog the public sewerage system with pure driven snow.

Comiski pushed through, made for the toilets. He opened the door of one stall and surprised two whiskery old men in overcoats sharing a pint of elderberry and a handful of mauve pills; they looked at him indignantly. He moved to the next stall, felt an edge of steel probe his right armpit. A hand grasped the back of his belt — the cop's favorite handle — hoisted him inside; it occurred to Comiski that in another fifteen seconds he would have made it.

He turned around, straddling the toilet, recognized the leather jacket, the tufts of eyebrow, the glove burns, and the malicious grin. Grunt held up the gun for his inspection;

Comiski found his navel covered by a nickel-plated automatic designed for a woman's purse and fitted with a length of perforated metal tubing that was welded inexpertly to the end of the barrel. There was a crease along the inside of the silencer.

"You do git around," Grunt said. He looked Comiski over, gestured toward the parcel. "Why don't you put that load on me, Dude? I'll mail it for you."

Comiski pulled the package out of his pocket and handed it across.

"Now let me out, punk," he said.

"Why all the aggression, Dude? I bet you plumb forgot it was me that turned you on that time. Now I'm gonna let you go, but first I got to make sure you ain't putting ole Grunt on. You'd be surprised how many spades nowadays are dealing in Aunt Jemima's."

Grunt cradled the automatic in the crook of his arm, tore the newspaper, and unrolled the plastic bag, thrust his fingers inside; he never stopped watching Comiski.

"Finger-lickin' good," Grunt said, raising the bag to his nose.

Comiski heard the bell ringing for the fourth race. It set off the alarm in his own brain: he remembered the day in the stables, the beating and the bruises — his loins still bore the hues of wilting flowers. Sex with Carrie was an autumnal act of pollination, a fortuitous conjunction before the big freeze. He was aware of the absurdity of his action, couldn't stop himself: he rammed the plastic bag with the flat of his hand, driving Grunt's head against the door. The pistol fired, jammed on the shell, and the toilet bowl between Comiski's legs shattered, spilling cold water over his shoes. He clubbed Grunt with

189

the bottom of his fist, knocking him to the floor. The gun lay between his outstretched legs, but Grunt didn't reach for it; he raised his fingers and touched his cheeks. A substance like sifted flour caked his hair and face and hands, crumbled and drifted down over his jacket and Levi's, sprinkled the surface of the water, and floated out beneath the partition of the stall. He looked up at Comiski with wide comic eyes, hoary lashes, his mouth a slash in the bottom of a tragedian's inflexible white mask.

Comiski retrieved the automatic, unlocked the door, and stepped over him. The two old men huddled against the wall opposite; there was no one else in the room except for Bud, who stood between him and the exit. Comiski showed him the gun before slipping it into his pocket, and Bud moved over by the urinals, watched him pass.

"You're picking up a lot of drag, Dude," he said.

Comiski went out. Two narcotics detectives stood on either side of the door; on the floor between them was Carrie's shopping bag, and one of them held a crumpled saffron dress in his hand.

"Well?" Comiski asked.

"Well, what?"

He removed the sunglasses. "Here I am. I'm all yours."

One of the detectives grinned. "Nobody wants you, Comiski."

Both men skirted him as if he were contaminated. As they went into the rest room, they hitched up their belts — the involuntary gesture of policemen who expect to be using their weapons.

Comiski limped down the stairs. Nobody wanted him:

he was free, held no promise, and posed no threats — a real period piece. He was retiring to his cell and his tube, his magazines and his paperback westerns, an occasional whore and his bourbon. That, certainly. The day of the ruminator was past; life seemed to require a commitment of which he was incapable. He wasn't feeding the Easy any longer.

He pushed through the turnstile, hailed a Yellow from the cabstand. A trash bin on the curb bore the picture of an insect with blood dripping from its jaws, and a slogan admonishing him as a litterbug. He dropped the sunglasses into the bin and was about to follow them with the automatic; the touch of the sculptured plastic handle stopped him. It was possible that no one wanted anyone — a problem of semantics, surely.

The driver swung open the door of the cab, but Comiski didn't get in. Instead, he turned and walked across the parking lot. The man cursed him, but Comiski didn't care; he found himself with a purpose, knew the odd blessing of lucidity. He was going to get the girl and they were simply going to leave. Light breaks, indeed.

His progress was marked by the soggy exhalations of wet shoes. A guard at the gate studied his press card and let him pass; the rutted expanse of mud and weeds was crowded with touring cars and trailers bearing out-of-state license plates, and Negro grooms hurried among the buildings with an air of frightened efficiency. No one noticed Comiski. He moved toward the stable — the old battleground — was challenged by a black man who stepped out from among the rosebushes lining the metal fence. Comiski stopped, waited for Tea's accomplice to disengage his flowered shirt from the thorns. A crude bandage covered one ear, caked with dried blood; he held a glass phial filled with a clear liquid.

"Hold it dare," he said, tearing the sleeve and freeing himself.

"I don't have it," Comiski told him. "Your bundle's gone." The man's eyes grew wide; he began to stammer.

"It doesn't matter," Comiski said. "The man with the money won't be there. Tea's plans didn't work out."

The Negro raised his hand. "I gwine burn you."

Comiski stepped around him, walked on. He was sweating again, not from fear but from anticipation: he looked forward to the concealing darkness of the stable, the defiance of memory and guilt. Wounds were insults; he was through with all that. With sudden clarity he recalled an early morning cab ride to the cemetery, barely a week before, and a dream that had haunted him ever since, censored by daylight, intertwined with the fantasies of sleep. Comiski was taking a trip, piloted by competent hands that drew him farther and farther from the sight of dawn and the day's routine; it promised to be a long and easy voyage.

He leaned against the sliding door. The smells were at him: dry straw and dust, blankets synonymous with fear — the scent of violence and degradation. Comiski stood for a moment in semi-darkness, waiting for his eyes to adjust, groped forward until he touched the rough wooden barrier. The nearest stalls were empty; from the far end of the stable came the whisper of wind in loose straw.

He called out. The sound was loud and incongruous, lost in shadow; the name sounded strange on his lips. He stumbled over a loaded wheelbarrow, pushed one hand down into soft powder. Cursing softly, he clapped his palms together; the smell of lye was choking.

Carrie's voice was close by and unmistakable: she yelled, "Hey!" and was stifled.

Comiski lunged forward, tearing the automatic out of his pocket. He struggled with the mechanism, failed to dislodge the spent shell; someone stepped out into the passageway, and he could see the outline of a blunt ugly revolver.

"Hold it right there."

He recognized Delaverne's drawl, his upright stance, his air of plodding competence; his face looked different in the gloom, devoid of expression. Comiski was about to speak when bits of straw showered down from the loft. He stepped back, fell over the wheelbarrow, instinctively raised the automatic to shield his face.

Hold it there.

You're here.

He looked up into the telescopic barrels of a shotgun that did not converge. Whether Delaveme or the cop in the rafters fired first, Comiski never knew.

A RED LIGHT hung in the night sky above Tulane Avenue. It blinked rapidly — a celestial cardiograph responding to the city's pulse, the eye of the Beholder affected by a tic — began to germinate, encircling the point of origin like Scorpio's jointed tail traced in neon, ended in the upthrust barb of an arrow. There the sun burst. Yellow and orange gases burned about the periphery; the interior glowed white, changed to lavender, died in deep purple. The message asserted itself in cool comforting blue: **HIDE-AWAY MOTEL AND LOUNGE**.

The sky went black again, punctuated by the point of angry

red light.

Carrie turned away before the routine was repeated. The spiral seemed to pull her toward its vertiginous center; she hadn't expected that sunburst. So sudden and so conclusive. The star's demise scored her retina; for several seconds she saw the purple disk transposed on the plate glass window of the Trailways bus station across the avenue. Carrie passed her hand before her face, closed her fingers on emptiness. The traffic ceased, opening her route of escape; she hefted the cardboard suitcase and stepped off the curb, concentrated on the swinging doors of the terminal.

It never let up: there could be no real change. She found herself straddling the yellow line, embroiled in the glare of headlights; a pink Oldsmobile convertible with a crumpled fender nudged the suitcase aside, while the driver — a muscular woman with limp white hair — shouted, "Crazy-ass nigger!" Carrie stared in amazement as the car pulled away. All these people were on to her, watching for her to make her move, waiting to cut her off; they never seemed to miss. She felt neither anger nor resentment, admired such savvy. How the word got around.

She gained the far curb, sat down on the suitcase to rest. A light rain mottled the pavement around her, touched her face and the backs of her hands, gently moving her along; two sailors in winter blues leaned against the wall, watching. Carrie smiled at them, shrugged her shoulders, but they just smoked their cheroots and stared, as if waiting for her to go through a soft-shoe routine, to lose heart and begin to scream. Her amazement grew: even the tourists were on to her.

She pushed back the sleeve of her sweater, massaged the

crusty flesh in the crook of her elbow, congratulated herself: that was finished. Her kit had been dumped into the wastepaper basket in a Texaco station rest room that afternoon, abandoned for good amid scrubbed white tiles and the antiseptic odor of liquid soap; it was the cleanest place Carrie could remember. During the rush she had knelt against the rim of the toilet seat, holding on to the basin, felt the room shift like an elevator descending a shaft of polished quartz, strung on silver cables threaded through the eye of the sun and washed in some golden petroleum product. A uniformed attendant was waiting when she stepped outside, and she thought he had come to serve her, that the two of them would go off arm in arm to a buffet of jellied meats and glazed pastry served on starched white linen. Thanksgiving. The attendant tried to kick her as she crossed the parking lot toward Dryades, fending him off with the suitcase; for once she didn't care.

Carrie had never felt so clean and so empty. When sleep came it would be easy and it would last for a long time.

She lifted the suitcase, pushed through the swinging doors. The terminal was crowded with black people lounging on long wooden benches, straddling valises like her own and shopping bags stuffed with clothes and food, cardboard boxes tied up with clothesline. Teen-age boys clustered around the pinball machine, jostled and abused it with ritualistic incantations; the room reeked of cigarette smoke and hot grease and unwashed bodies. The juke box in the adjacent hash house pounded through the lyrics of "Bend It." A loud-speaker transmitted a sexless voice intoning the names of southern Louisiana towns as if they belonged to another world. "Bogaloosa, Baton Rouge," the voice concluded, "and points west."

Carrie moved warily along the row of lockers. She accepted the stares of her own people as natural: they would be the first to spot her — a crazy-ass nigger. It seemed like a harsh judgment. After years of messing up the view, she deserved more respect; they must concede that she was capable of riling Whitey's overfed guts — shaking up all that Southern Comfort. But no one seemed to realize this. She saw herself not as a menace but as a curiosity: it didn't seem right.

A white clerk with sculptured hair stood at the counter. Behind him was a board crowded with bus schedules; letters and digits swarmed through Carrie's mind, produced a murmur of frantic wings. She had to pick a place, a territory, her own piece of the universe: it was a terrifying decision. She tried to imagine herself as part of Mandeville, Texarkana, Tulsa; the idea of being Yazoo City made her shudder. The clerk smiled at her, waited patiently for the big choice. The shoulders of his gabardine jacket were dusted with dandruff — driven snow. The day threatened to last forever.

"How much is Chicago?" Carrie asked.

"Chicargo *Illinoise?*"

She unstuck her tongue from her palate, had to think it out.

"That's the one," she said.

"Twenty-six dollars twenty-five cents."

Carrie listened to the scaly wings, faltered: all those numbers.

"What about St. Louis?"

"Twenty-two ninety-five."

"You sure got it all down."

"We have to be speedy." He was still smiling.

196

"Give me Memphis, then."

"Fourteen forty. Departure in twenty minutes. Arrival two-twelve pee em."

She moistened her lips, tried to calculate. Surely she could afford Memphis.

"That's one way, of course," the clerk said. "Seems everybody's going one way."

"It's the only way to travel."

Carrie pushed fifteen dollars across the counter. Her money didn't seem to buy much: Memphis was right between nowhere and somewhere, but at least it was north — she was climbing.

He gave her the change and her ticket. "Thank ya vera much. You have yourself a good trip."

"It's already started," Carrie said.

She pushed the suitcase across the floor toward the benches. That was going to be the longest twenty minutes of her life: a kind of atonement before deliverance, the last hassle of being nowhere. She was exasperated by the unwieldiness of Tea's old suitcase; she ought to know what she was transporting.

She sat down next to a black man in a Stetson who kept wiping his face with a blue silk handkerchief. Carrie straddled the suitcase, manipulated the lock. Tea had nothing worth hiding; the idea of examining his few possessions was exciting. He might have left something just for her: a trinket, a message, some tribute to what was, after all, a kind of love. The flimsy cardboard yielded beneath the pressure of her thumbs, and the latch sprang loose; she opened the suitcase, and the entire room seemed to fill with the sweetish odor of decay. It was a childhood smell, like that of malt syrup and spring water

197

fermenting in her father's earthen crock beneath the porch, where he put up homemade beer in Nehi bottles; she couldn't make it out. The suitcase was stuffed with soiled clothes. Tea's loose-leaf notebook lay on top, next to a matchbox bound with a rubber band; she placed them next to her on the bench, delved into the rags, uncovered a *Who's Who in America* stolen from the Loyola Street library and something large and oval wrapped in stained newspaper. Carrie stared at it, marveled at the fact that she was neither afraid nor disgusted, but disappointed: not exactly the tribute she expected. She always knew Tea was absent-minded; the police would call it criminal negligence. No way to treat a sugar daddy.

"Hey, Parks," she said aloud. "How come you swung so low?"

There was no answer. The man in the Stetson began to snuffle, held the silk handkerchief over his nose; Carrie noticed that the people on the bench opposite were watching her. Very carefully she closed the suitcase, mashed the latch back in place, took it, the notebook, and the matchbox, and moved off toward the lockers lining the terminal wall. The things people did, the things they forgot to do: it was enough to break you.

Carrie deposited her quarter, opened the door, and shoved the suitcase into the vault. Not much of a ceremony, she thought, but at least the place was dry. Tea always said Parks was an artifact; that was no excuse.

The loudspeaker said, "Your attention please," and Carrie turned to see two white men in dark suits coming for her. She pressed the notebook against her breasts, grinning stupidly, waiting for them to strike. The police were complicating themselves: they wasted Tea, which was natural, but then they killed Comiski. Carrie couldn't figure that out, remembered poor soft white Andrew lying in the straw, one hand draping the handle of the overturned wheelbarrow, the air full of dust; everyone except Comiski was coughing. The cop in the rafters never used his shotgun, seemed afraid to climb down. The other one told her to move along, and she heard his teeth chattering; somebody made a mistake, he said, and Carrie said she never bothered about remembering mistakes. As if she wanted to stay, as if she had a pressing social engagement.

The two men looked contemptuously at her hair and her bare feet, went into the restaurant; hugging the wall, Carrie hurried toward the women's rest room. The voice from the loud-speaker followed her inside. She stood before a mirror and touched her hair, examined that scrawny girl with drawn waxen skin and sunken eyes: she couldn't blame Tea for not wanting to ball, the way she let herself go. Instinctively she felt in her sweater pocket for lipstick, touched the change, the residue of the whole scene and the promise of the future: 35 cents and a ticket to Memphis.

Carrie wanted to cry, seemed to have lost the knack. Even at the morgue she couldn't get it up: the tears weren't there. *You want a member...* She moaned, clawed at her face. She needed some connection, something solid with which to identify — some artifact; already she was forgetting. Eagerly she unwound the rubber band and opened the matchbox, found it contained only rusted razor blades — no help there. The notebook was her last chance, and Carrie shrank from that responsibility: she had never understood that black man's jive, couldn't cope with the theories. Now they were all she had.

She reluctantly opened the notebook on the edge of the

basin and thumbed through it.... *direct action liberates. To kill — decisive, ultimate commit/ no retreat.* She expected as much: how that man could carry on. Her eyes skimmed over the last page, read the final entry: *Sis & Whitey no excuse Hold on No excuse no important no explain / no exist*

Carrie was afraid. Carefully she reread the passage; the script was barely legible, thin and harried, as if it had been written in bad light by someone in a state of exhaustion. The absence of punctuation seemed to denude the words, lent them the reality of harsh truthful ranting. *No excuse no important no explain.* So that was it: Tea knew about Comiski, after all, that was why he never came for her, why she never saw him again.

Carrie cringed from the light and the sight of herself. An immense Negro woman in a transparent plastic raincoat stopped bullying the towel machine and watched her, continued to snatch at bits of paper towel. The Voice was talking again.

No exist.

Carrie picked up one of the razor blades, went into a stall, and locked the door behind her. She bent over the toilet and pressed the blade against her neck. No matter how bad things got, you never quite made it — there always seemed to be something worse just around the bend. A weird kind of hope. She tried, couldn't get the blade to work; still, she had to get around the problem of Tea. Carrie could prove that she existed: she could thwart him as she had done before — she could betray him again. And again and again. Desecration was the only way to keep the memory going; she wasn't strong enough for the alternative sort of tribute. Tea was never one for praise, thrived on humiliation and rage. The way things turned out.

Carrie hacked savagely with the razor blade. When she emerged from the stall, the woman in the plastic raincoat said, "Girl, you crazy?" In the mirror Carrie glimpsed the short uneven burr that made her own eyes look huge and jaundiced; shorn hair clung to her sweater like clots of dead Spanish moss.

She walked out into the glare of the terminal lights. The Voice said, "... *Jackson, Granada, Memphis, and points north,*" and she found her bus waiting in the aquatic glow of the arc lamps, the windows glazed black — a mercy ship foundered upon a shoal of impoverished luggage, sprinkled with warm dark rain. She took her place in line, the ticket clamped in her fist, felt herself begin to drift. The bus driver looked at her with contempt, shrank from contact with her fingers as she offered him the slip of paper and mounted the steps.

There was an empty seat by the window, next to a wizened white woman whose hands were folded on her *Readers Digest*. She looked at Carrie through steel-rimmed spectacles, her gray eyes revealing neither hostility nor acquiescence: she was waiting for the play. All you have to do is push across and take a pew — you've got to move or you'll be standing up from now on. But there was something about the old woman's eyes that held her — the patient disdain. Carrie felt her life beginning all over again: Lord, the way things turned out.

A man carrying a briefcase shouldered past and took the empty seat; Carrie moved to the back of the bus. People stood in the aisle, crowded together like cattle, waiting for the journey to begin. She found herself hemmed in by the black man wearing the Stetson. The bus shuddered as the motor turned over; she almost fell as it lurched out into Tulane

Avenue, saw the neon sunburst for the last time. Liquor stores, bars, and bondsmen's offices slipped by like miniature grottoes in a dirty aquarium. The police station loomed in the murk and was left behind.

She had forgotten Tea's notebook. It was lying open on the edge of the washbasin, exposed to the eyes of all women — white and black — who wore plastic raincoats. That was too much: it went beyond blasphemy. She pushed against the mass of flesh separating her from the front of the bus. She would make the driver stop and turn back; she opened her mouth to voice her demands — her rights — but no sound came out.

She closed her eyes, held on to the back of the seat, fought the undertow toward rest and oblivion: she had to see it out. When she opened her eyes again, the bus was speeding across the Pontchartrain Causeway, and she glimpsed the blue lights along the lake's edge — the watery limits of the city's drag.

Carrie rested her head against the broad back of the man in the Stetson, caught the odors of ashes and sweat. She was past it now. Jostled by unfamiliar bodies, rocked by the motion of the bus, and lulled by hushed voices, she sped northward into darkness, asleep on her feet.

Made in United States
Orlando, FL
24 May 2025

61548783R00122